ALAMO WARS

RAY VILLAREAL

PIÑATA BOOKS
ARTE PÚBLICO PRESS
HOUSTON, TEXAS

Alamo Wars is funded in part by grants from the City of Houston through the Houston Arts Alliance and by the Exemplar Program, a program of Americans for the Arts in collaboration with the LarsonAllen Public Services Group, funded by the Ford Foundation.

Piñata Books are full of surprises!

Piñata Books

An imprint of
Arte Público Press
University of Houston
452 Cullen Performance Hall
Houston, Texas 77204-2004

Cover illustration by Gary Swimmer and Giovanni Mora
Cover design by Mora Des!gn

Villareal, Ray.
    Alamo Wars / by Ray Villareal.
        p.   cm.
    Summary: When a Texas school puts on an original play about the Alamo, the students and teachers confront modern conflicts about history, identity, and the meaning of courage.
    ISBN: 978-1-55885-513-7
    1. Mexican Americans—Juvenile fiction. [1. Mexican Americans—Fiction. 2. Bullies—Fiction. 3. Prejudices—Fiction. 4. Theater—Fiction. 5. Schools—Fiction. 6. Texas—History—Revolution, 1835-1836—Fiction.] I. Title.
PZ7.V718AI 2008
[Fic]—dc22
                                                                  2007047466
                                                                  CPI

8 9 0 1 2 3 4 5 6 7   10 9 8 7 6 5 4 3 2 1

DEDICATION

For the 1992-1993 fourth grade teachers and students
at Rosemont School in Dallas

"Remember the Alamo!"

CHAPTER ONE

The problems started when Miss Josephine McKeever died.

Miss Mac, as she was called, had taught English at Rosemont Middle School for fifty-one years, almost as long as the school had existed. She never married and refused to use the title Ms.

"Sounds like a mosquito buzzing in someone's ear," she would say.

Although she had become eligible to retire seventeen years earlier, Miss Mac continued to teach, despite growing health problems that any seventy-three-year-old woman could expect to have. So devoted was she to her profession that her coworkers sometimes joked that Miss Mac would die in the classroom.

One afternoon, during her planning period, while she sat at her desk grading papers, a sharp, fiery pain zipped up her left arm. It exploded in her chest. Miss Mac jerked her head up, clasped her hands over her heart, and collapsed in her chair.

When her students arrived a short while later, they discovered their teacher slouched in her seat. Her head was tilted back. Her eyes were closed, and her mouth was wide open. The kids giggled, thinking she'd fallen asleep. Several times before, they'd come to class, and discovered her sleeping in her chair.

Raquel Flores urged Marco Díaz to nudge Miss Mac awake, but Marco refused. He didn't want to be the one responsible for waking her up to a classroom full of laughter and humiliation.

No one tried to wake her up. Instead, the kids took their seats. They pretended to work on their book reports, all the while trying to stifle their laughter.

Billy Ray Cansler, who sat at the front desk of the third row, wadded a sheet of notebook paper. He handed it to Luther Bowers who sat across from him. Billy Ray dared Luther to toss it into the teacher's mouth.

"Come on," Billy Ray whispered. "Five bucks if you make a basket."

Luther giggled nervously. He glanced up at Miss Mac's open mouth. It was certainly an inviting target. From where he sat, he was sure he could sink it.

Two points!

Luther imagined the teacher waking up, gagging, with a ball of paper stuck in her mouth. It would be a laugh riot! He'd be the talk of the school for days.

But Miss Mac would know he'd done it. Even if none of the other kids squealed on him, which was unlikely, especially with Myra "The Fastest Mouth in the West" Coonrod in his class, she'd know. Just like she'd known that he and Billy Ray were the ones who'd been flooding the boys' bathrooms.

Luther and Billy Ray had been cramming toilet paper rolls down the commodes and then flushing them, spilling streams of water onto the floor and out into the hallways.

No one had seen them do it; Luther was almost positive of it. Because even after Mr. Rathburn, the principal, announced that he was offering a twenty-five-dollar reward to anyone who could help him catch the person or persons responsible for flooding the bathrooms, no one came forward to collect the money.

Yet somehow Miss Mac knew he and Billy Ray were the culprits. Even in a school with almost seven hundred potential suspects, she zeroed in on the two of them. She didn't come right out and accuse them of flooding the bathrooms. But when she addressed the problem to her seventh graders, her wide, hazel eyes bore down on Luther and Billy Ray the whole time she spoke.

"Mischievous minds, like idle hands, are the devil's tools," Miss Mac proclaimed, delivering one of her trademark fire-and-brimstone sermons. "The vandals think they are clever. They think they have gotten away with their misdeeds, but . . . 'Vengeance is mine, saith the Lord!'" She wagged a long, bony finger, like a conductor's baton, first at Billy Ray, then at Luther.

After that, Miss Mac moved them to the front desks in the second and third rows. And neither one of them was allowed to go to the bathroom alone, not even if they claimed it was an emergency. They had to wait until class was over to do their business.

"Ten bucks!" Billy Ray goaded, hiking the offer. "Ten bucks if you can knock it in." He held out ten fingers in front of Luther's face.

Luther was giddy. Ten dollars was a lot of money, and he knew Billy Ray was good for it.

Luther stared at Miss Mac. She looked as if she was leaning back in a dentist's chair, with the dentist standing over her, telling her to say *ah* while he got ready to yank out her tooth.

Luther squeezed the paper ball tightly in his hand. His tongue slid out of the corner of his mouth, like a snail peeking out of its shell.

"Do it, Luther!" Billy Ray commanded. "C'mon, do it. Do it now!"

Whether Luther would have actually shot the wadded paper ball into Miss Mac's mouth, Billy Ray never got the chance to find out. Because at the moment he said, *Do it now!* Mrs. Frymire, the science teacher, stepped into the classroom. She had spotted her unconscious colleague from the hallway.

As soon as she entered, the class roared with laughter and pointed at their teacher.

Mrs. Frymire smiled weakly. She gave Miss Mac's arm a gentle tug. "Wake up, dear," she called in a soft voice.

Miss Mac's head lolled from one side to the other.

The class howled.

Mrs. Frymire let out a nervous chuckle. "Miss Mac? Your students are here." She took her by the shoulder and gave her a firm shake.

When Miss Mac's limp body failed to respond, a dawning horror filled Mrs. Frymire's face.

"Miss Mac? Oh, my . . . Miss Mac!"

She recoiled, as if she'd been stung by a bee.

The kids' grins quickly melted as they finally realized, to their dismay, what had happened to their teacher.

Raquel Flores's face drained of color as she stared at the lifeless body.

Myra Coonrod sat at her desk, gawking, her eyeballs bulging out like goose eggs, her mouth as wide open as Miss Mac's.

Luther Bowers gaped in stunned silence. A wave of nausea swept up from the pit of his stomach. It rose up his throat. Luther bolted from his seat and scrambled to the back of the room, sure that he was going to puke at any moment.

Billy Ray Cansler sprang from his chair and joined him.

Mrs. Frymire, having initially panicked at the grisly discovery, now regained her composure. Trying to hold back her tears, she told the class, "Boys and girls, I . . . I'd like for all of you to step into the hallway . . . and line up . . . outside my room."

"Is . . . is Miss Mac . . . ?" Raquel Flores started, but the words refused to come out.

CHAPTER TWO

Miss Mac's funeral service was held on Saturday morning at ten o'clock at the West Cliff Baptist Church. Hundreds of mourners, many of them former students, filled the sanctuary. Dozens more spilled into the foyer.

The pastor, the Reverend Jimmy Hodges, praised Miss Mac for her "many years of commitment and dedication to the Lord's work at West Cliff Baptist." She had served as church pianist, Sunday school teacher, and, more recently, head of the senior citizens' group, the ADM — Age Doesn't Matter.

A Power Point presentation highlighting Miss Mac's fifty-one-year teaching career was shown on a large screen set up in front of the baptistry.

Grieving soon gave way to heart-warming smiles. Tears of sorrow were transformed into tears of joy as pictures of Miss Mac flashed before the congregation.

There was Miss Mac, playing the piano during a seventh-grade Christmas program she directed. Miss Mac, helping her students into their costumes as they prepared to present an original play she had written called "Medusa's Bad Hair Day." Miss Mac, dressed as a giant pencil as part of a campaign to encourage writing. Miss Mac, at bat in a softball game between the teachers and the students. Miss Mac, posing with several Dallas Cowboys players when they visited the school.

After the service, Mr. Rathburn assembled the teachers in the church parking lot. "I'd like for us to do something special at school to honor Miss Mac's memory," he told the group.

"Absolutely," Mrs. Pruitt, the Texas history teacher, agreed. "What did you have in mind?"

Mr. Rathburn pulled a handkerchief from his coat pocket and took a couple of swipes at his nose. "Nothing in particular. I'm open to suggestions."

"How about a plaque with her name?" Mr. Watts, the math teacher, offered. "You know, in loving memory of . . . or something like that. We could hang it in the office or in the teachers' lounge."

"Oh, come on, Barry," Mrs. Frymire said scornfully. "We can certainly do better than that. After all, she did give fifty-one years of service to the school."

"Hey, don't jump down my throat, Doris. It was just a thought."

Mrs. Pruitt's face lit up. "I have an idea. Why don't we name the auditorium in her honor? I mean, after all those wonderful stage productions she presented in there, I think it would be very appropriate. We could call it . . . The Josephine McKeever Memorial Auditorium."

The teachers turned to Mr. Rathburn.

His bespectacled eyes twinkled. "I think that's an outstanding idea, Claire. I like it." He pulled the handkerchief from his pocket and blew a trumpet blast from his nose. "It'll probably have to be okayed by the superintendent and the school board, but I don't think we'll have any problems."

Rosemont School did not offer drama classes as part of its curriculum. Miss Mac had taken it upon herself to create an after-school theater arts program.

"It's an extension of my English class, a visible expression of what the children are reading," she explained when she asked for permission to establish the program. Miss Mac had no formal theater arts background, but one would hardly have noticed. The year before, she presented Shakespeare's *A Midsummer Night's Dream*. The show was slated as a one-night-only performance. But due to the overwhelmingly positive response it received, it was presented twice more, to a packed auditorium each night.

"The Josephine McKeever Memorial Auditorium," Mrs. Frymire said. Her eyes grew misty. "It sounds beautiful."

"We could still hang a plaque on the outside of the auditorium," Mr. Watts said. "You know, in loving memory of . . ."

CHAPTER THREE

On Monday after school, Mrs. Frymire began clearing out Miss Mac's room. Bookcases, overflowing with fifty-one years of books, lined the walls of the classroom.

Mrs. Frymire wondered if it would be better to simply leave the books behind for the new teacher. She quickly dismissed the thought. At the funeral she spoke with Rose Adderly, Miss Mac's sister. Mrs. Frymire promised she would box all of Miss Mac's belongings and deliver them to her. It would be up to Rose Adderly to decide what would become of the books.

Mrs. Frymire folded the flaps of a box shut and stacked it against the wall with the twelve others that had been filled so far. She stretched her aching back. Her arms, too, were sore from all the heavy lifting. Mr. Watts, Mrs. Pruitt, and some other teachers had offered to help, but Mrs. Frymire kindly turned them down. She wanted to do this alone.

She walked to the back of the room and sank into Miss Mac's brown, overstuffed rocker. It was an old chair Miss Mac had bought at a flea market.

Mrs. Frymire rocked back and forth, recalling the many times she had passed by her beloved friend's room. She'd often seen Miss Mac sitting in this chair, her students listening quietly, while she read aloud to them.

Mrs. Frymire stopped rocking. Her eyes filled with tears as the realization sank in that she would never again see her friend.

Twenty-seven years ago, Mrs. Frymire began her teaching career at Rosemont School. Miss Mac was the first teacher she met. Being a teacher had been a greater challenge than Mrs. Frymire had ever anticipated back when she was in college. It was Miss Mac who helped her survive that first year. She became her mentor and friend.

When Mrs. Frymire married, Miss Mac served as her maid of honor. Later, when her two children were born, Miss Mac regularly visited the house to babysit.

Mrs. Frymire tilted her head upward and closed her eyes. "I'm going to miss you, Miss Mac," she muttered through her tears.

After a while, she sat up. She surveyed the room, taking inventory of the unfinished work. There were still piles of books that needed to be packed. Some wall decorations had to come down. Miss Mac's desk would have to be cleaned out.

Mrs. Frymire glanced at the gray file cabinet standing behind the desk. She decided to work on that next. Otherwise, she might forget to empty it later. She opened the cabinet drawers and sifted through the file folders. They contained a large surplus of teaching ideas. Certainly Miss Mac's sister wouldn't want them, she thought. Mrs. Frymire decided to save the materials for the new teacher.

It was then that Mrs. Frymire made an intriguing discovery. A crumpled manila folder from the bottom drawer caught her eyes. She drew it out and skimmed through its contents. She smiled. *This is it! This is how we'll honor Miss Mac's memory.*

CHAPTER FOUR

Krak-a-tah! Krak-a-tah! Krak-a-tah!

The old man leaned forward on his cane. His glasses hung at the tip of his puffy nose. His craggy white brows bounced up and down, matching the beat of the speed bag.

Krak-a-tah! Krak-a-tah! Krak-a-tah!

"Can you feel the rhythm, Marco?" he shouted in a raspy voice. "Dance with it. There you go. That's it. 1-2-3! 1-2-3! 1-2-3!"

Krak-a-tah! Krak-a-tah! Krak-a-tah!

Marco Díaz followed the cadence of the black speed bag. He drove his fists into it with swift, well-timed punches.

"Make smaller, circling movements," the old man dictated. "Swing smaller! There you go. Now pick up the pace. *¡Con más ganas!*"

Marco revved up his punches. The speed bag was now a rapid, rebounding blur against his gloves.

Satisfied, the old man relaxed with his back against the bench. He sat his cane on his lap and watched Marco work the black bag with a flurry of punches.

Unaware that he was doing it, the old man clenched his withered hands and jabbed the air, following the beat of the bag.

Krak-a-tah! Krak-a-tah! Krak-a-tah!

His mind traveled back to November of 1956.

That was when he'd fought in the most important boxing match of his career. It was on the undercard of the Patterson/Moore world heavyweight title fight in Chicago.

Other than his parents and his trainers, no one had gone to see him fight. He was unknown to most of the boxing world. The fans who flocked to Chicago Stadium that night had paid their money to see the brash, twenty-one-year-old Floyd Patterson fight against the aging, light-heavyweight champion, Archie Moore. Patterson and Moore were battling for the heavyweight title that had been vacated by Rocky Marciano.

The old man, who at the time was known as Anthony "El Águila" Dávila, was scheduled to fight Paul "Pinkie" Rosario in a middleweight bout.

Anthony "El Águila" Dávila was undefeated. He had a 14 and 0 record with eleven knockouts. And after his bout with Rosario, he expected to be 15 and 0 with twelve knockouts. Then he'd be in line for a title fight against the world middleweight champion, Sugar Ray Robinson. And after he beat Sugar Ray Robinson, the whole world would know who he was.

Pinkie Rosario, on the other hand, was entering the ring with an unimpressive record of 7 wins and 9 losses and no one offering him any hope that he could defeat the up-and-coming "El Águila."

Theirs was the first bout on the card.

Many of the fans were still filing in, trying to find their seats, when the match started. Some were at the concession stands buying beer, sodas, and popcorn.

The introductions took longer than the fight.

As soon as the bell sounded, Pinkie Rosario rushed toward an unprepared Dávila. He attacked him with three quick jabs, followed by a straight right hand. Dávila tried to fight back, but Rosario was too quick, too strong. A left, right, left combination, punctuated with a thundering uppercut, sent a stunned Dávila crashing to the mat, eighteen seconds into the fight.

While the referee counted, Dávila, stupidly bewildered, staggered to his feet.

He should have stayed down.

Rosario hit him with a left hook, then a straight right. Dávila collapsed on the canvas like a house of cards. This time he did not get up until after the referee had counted to ten, the bell had rung, and Rosario's arm had been raised in victory.

For Anthony "El Águila" Dávila, there would be no 15 and 0 record. There would be no match for the middleweight championship title against Sugar Ray Robinson.

And the world would not know who he was.

Following his humiliating defeat at the hands of Pinkie Rosario, Dávila lost three of his next five fights. He never recovered from the fact that on the night that should've been his, he lost by knockout to an unheralded boxer with a mediocre record. To a fighter with the unlikely nickname of "Pinkie."

After a loss to a journeyman boxer with a worse record than Pinkie Rosario, Dávila hung up his gloves and left the sport for good. That is, until Marco came along.

Krak-a-tah! Krak-a-tah! Krak-a-tah!

The old man's face beamed with a gratifying smile. "That's good, Marco. That's real good. You can take a break now."

Marco smacked the speed bag with a final, solid punch. The bag swung back and forth before teetering to a stop. He sat on the bench next to the old man who tossed him a towel that had once been white but was now the color of wallpaper paste.

"Thanks, Grandpa."

Marco threw the towel over his shoulder. He pulled off his training gloves, gripping them with his armpits, and tossed them on the bench next to his grandfather. Then he mopped up the sweat that was leaking from his forehead. He grabbed his nearly empty water bottle and squirted the rest of its contents into his mouth. Marco stretched his long legs on the floor as he watched Mickey O'Donnell and another teenager trade punches in the boxing ring. In the corner, Bryce Dixon worked the dummy bag with exacting, savage shots. Santos Estrada lay on a wrestling mat, doing sit-ups to tighten his stomach muscles.

"I want you to take the rope and practice skip jumping for a while," the old man said.

Marco groaned. "Grandpa, do I have to? I'm tired."

"Grandpa, do I have to? I'm tired," the old man mimicked in a high voice. "You're too young to be tired, boy. You can say 'I'm tired' when you're old, like me. You think I used to cry 'I'm tired' when I was in the ring? How do you expect to be a champion if you start whining 'I'm tired' after every workout? Now, go get the rope. And I don't want you jumping around like a kiddy garden girl, either."

Marco sighed. He sucked in a deep breath of air, then let it rush out. "Okay, Grandpa."

He knew not to disagree with the old man. And not just out of respect. His grandfather never backed down from an argument. He could babble nonstop on any topic, until he felt satisfied that he had gotten his point across.

"Grandpa can talk the devil into buying a box of matches," Marco's mother would say.

Marco picked up the rope. He whipped it around his body, alternating between one foot and the other. Skipping rope had been part of his training since he was eight years old, when his grandfather first brought him to the East Grand Boxing Club to teach him how to box.

Marco's mother had been against letting her son get involved with boxing from the beginning, and she let her father know it.

"You're trying to relive your life through him, Papi, and I'm not going to let you do it," she had said.

Not about to be dissuaded, the old man decided to work on Marco's father instead.

"You don't want Marco to spend his life working in a body shop like you, do you, Frank?"

Marco's father was an auto-body repairman at the Maximum Motors Body Shop.

"Ain't nothing wrong with what I do, Tony. It's good work, and it pays the bills."

"Think of it, though," the old man said. "Marco could be the world champ some day. His name could be up in lights. He'd be up there with Muhammad Ali, Sugar Ray Leonard, Oscar De la Hoya, and Julio César Chávez. He'd be on ESPN, HBO, Showtime, and all the pay-per-views. And I can guarantee you, Frank, when Marco's making millions, he won't just say 'It pays the bills.' He'll be rolling in dough."

After that, and against his wife's wishes, Frank agreed to let his father-in-law teach Marco the basics of boxing.

Marco was now preparing to enter his third Golden Gloves Boxing Tournament.

He switched rope-jumping techniques, from the alternate foot-to-foot to a side straddle, then to an arm criss-cross. Skipping rope, he knew, would help him develop the coordination, balance, and speed he'd need when he got in the ring.

His grandfather shifted uncomfortably on the bench. His prosthetic leg had been bothering him. He'd had the same one for almost five years. Time to get it replaced. His left leg, the victim of his diabetes, had been amputated years ago. His eyesight was another casualty of the disease. It had begun to go out, flickering in spurts, like a battery on its last charge. He hoped his eyesight would hold out long enough to let him see Marco turn pro.

He massaged his knee and was about to remove his artificial limb when Raquel Flores and Izzy Peña arrived.

Marco stopped jumping.

"Hello, Grandpa," Raquel and Izzy greeted the old man. They called him "Grandpa" because that's what Marco called him.

"Hola, chamacos. ¿Cómo están?"

"Bien, gracias."

Izzy asked Marco, "You ready?"

Marco looked at his grandfather.

His grandfather stared at him for a moment. "Yeah, go ahead. I think we covered enough for today."

Marco grabbed the towel and swabbed his face and neck.

Grandpa leaned back on the bench and raised his prosthetic leg up to Izzy's waist. "Here, help me take this off."

Izzy looked at Marco with uncertainty.

"*Ándale, muchacho.* My knee hurts, and I'm having a hard time removing my leg."

Marco turned his head so Izzy couldn't see that he was trying to hold back a laugh.

Izzy gripped Grandpa's artificial leg and gave it a gentle tug.

"Harder!" Grandpa ordered. "It doesn't come off that easy."

Izzy pulled with greater force.

"Harder!"

Izzy clamped both hands firmly on the leg and yanked it.

As his artificial leg separated from his knee, Grandpa blew out a long, loud fart.

"*Aaah!* That felt *so* good." A contented smile spread across his face.

Raquel giggled.

Izzy's face flushed red.

"Sorry, Iz . . . I was going to tell you . . . " Marco couldn't get the words out, he was laughing so hard.

Izzy glared at him, then he laughed, too.

Grandpa gazed up with an innocent look on his face. "What'd I do?"

Marco's laughter eased long enough to explain to Raquel and Izzy, "That's Grandpa's version of 'Pull My Finger.'"

Izzy, still holding the prosthetic leg, asked, "What do you want me to do with this?"

"Gimme that." Grandpa snatched the leg away from Izzy's hands. "I need it for my new job. You know I got a new job, don't you, Marco?"

Marco had already heard this one, so he ignored him. Grandpa asked Raquel, "You wanna know where I'm working?"

"Where?"

"At IHOP." The old man roared with laughter. "Get it? *I hop!*"

Marco groaned. "Very funny, Grandpa. We're leaving. You want us to walk you home or anything?"

"Nah. My girlfriend's gonna meet me here. She also has one leg. Wanna know what her name is?"

Marco had already heard this one, too.

"Her name's Ilene. Get it? *I lean.*"

That one made Izzy and Raquel snicker.

"Don't encourage him," Marco said. "He can keep this up all day."

"Hey, you wanna know what to say to a one-legged hitchhiker?" Grandpa continued. "Hop in! Get it? Hop in!"

"See you, Grandpa," Marco said.

"Yeah, we'll see you, Grandpa," Raquel and Izzy added.

"What does a one-legged turkey say?" Grandpa called out as they exited the East Grand Boxing Club.

When Marco shut the door, he heard his grandfather's voice yell, "Hobble-Hobble!"

CHAPTER FIVE

When they arrived at the construction site, Izzy's little sister Blanca popped out from behind a tall yellow crane.

"Izzy! Marco! Raquel! Come here, quick! It ran toward the sand pile."

"What are you doing?" Izzy scolded. "You know you're not supposed to play here."

"I'm trying to catch the cabbit! Come on. Hurry, before it runs away." Blanca motioned with her hand for them to follow her. She sprinted toward the sand pile that sat next to the hulking steel frame, which in a few months would become the new offices for the Lone Star Life Insurance Company.

She stopped at the foot of the mound. She glanced up and saw a white, furry figure escaping down the side. It ran to a wooden fence and slipped underneath.

"Aw, it got away." Blanca gave the sand a swift kick.

"What was it?" Marco asked.

Izzy shook his head. "*Nada. Un gato.* Blanca's been trying to catch it for the past week or so."

"It's not a cat!" Blanca protested. "It's a cabbit."

"A what?" Marco wasn't sure he'd heard right.

"A cabbit," Blanca repeated. "*Un gatonejo.* That's what Tío Beto calls it."

With a smirk on his face, Izzy said, "Blanca thinks she's discovered an animal that's part cat, part rabbit. It showed up at our house one day, and she fed it some leftovers. Now it comes around every once in a while look-ing for more food. She's been trying to make it her pet, but it's just a dirty old cat."

Blanca frowned. "No, it's not. It has long ears and a bunny tail, and it hops like a rabbit but meows like a cat. It's a cabbit."

"Well, it didn't hop away, that's for sure," Izzy said. "It took off running like . . . like a scaredy-*cat*." He laughed. "Anyway, Mami doesn't want you playing any-where near the construction site. You need to go home."

"What about you? You're not supposed to play out here, either." Blanca was not about to be shooed away so easily.

"Yeah, but I'm older than you are," Izzy said. "I know how to take care of myself."

"Two years isn't that much older," Blanca argued.

Marco bent down in a crouch. He rested his hands on Blanca's shoulders and met her eyes. "*¿Sábes qué,* Blanca? I'll bet you the cabbit ran back to your house. He's waiting there for you right now. He probably wants you to give him something to eat."

Blanca's face brightened. That made sense. "You're right. Thanks, Marco. I'll see you at home, Izzy," she said and ran off.

"Don't tell Mami where I am," Izzy yelled.

Blanca didn't reply. She headed down the sidewalk and turned the corner to the next block.

"Thanks for helping me get rid of her," Izzy said. "She can be a real pest sometimes."

"Blanca's okay," Marco said with a shrug.

Izzy snorted. "Easy for you to say. She's not your sis-ter."

The workers had called it quits for the day. They usually did around four-thirty. Marco, Izzy, and Raquel liked to hang around at the construction site.

They had followed the building of the insurance company from the beginning, ever since the Nolan Park Apartments had been demolished to make room for the new offices.

They watched a wrecking ball pulverize the old dilapidated apartment complex, tearing down walls as if they were made out of papier-mâché. Later, bulldozers dug their claws into the ground and tore up the soil. Fat concrete trucks then poured the cement foundation. After the steel girders and beams were added, Marco and Izzy decided the structure would be perfect for climbing. Tons better than the monkey bars at the elementary school.

Raquel leaned against the crane and watched them scale up the building. She was tempted to join them, but she resisted. It wasn't because she was scared of heights. When she lived in Bustamante, Nuevo León, Mexico, she often hiked up the Cabeza de León Mountain with her father. She had also climbed up the steep slippery hills of the Grutas del Palmito cave on numerous occasions to enjoy the stalagmite and stalactite formations of El Castillo, Salón del Baile, and El King Kong.

But now that she was almost thirteen and living in the United States, climbing anything other than stairs seemed, well, undignified.

Raquel liked Marco. She had a huge crush on him. Of course she'd never tell him that. She'd never tell anybody, not even her cousin, Luisa. But she wrote about him in her diary.

I watched Marco working out at the gym today, she jotted in Spanish in one of many entries she had included about him. *He had his sleeves on his T-shirt rolled up. His muscles looked huge on his sweaty arms. ¡Qué guapo!*

She had wanted to get to know Marco since the first day of school, when she noticed him in her English and Texas history classes, but she was too nervous to approach him. Her lucky break came when she discovered that her father worked with Marco's father at the Maximum Motors Body Shop. She went to the shop one Saturday afternoon to take her father the lunch bag that he'd forgotten at home. There, she ran into Marco. They struck up a conversation and from then on became good friends.

Raquel hoped that some day they could become more than friends. For now, though, she was happy hanging out with him.

Marco and Izzy stopped in the middle of one of the beams and peered down. The sand pile rested about twelve feet below them.

Marco hesitated for a moment. Then he leaped into the air.

"Yeehaah!"

He landed with a soft thud, his feet sinking deep into the coarse sand, and rolled down the hill. Izzy jumped after him. Hitting the mound, he spiraled downward until he rested next to Marco. They rose, climbed up to the second story, and jumped off again. They jumped twice more. Finally, they joined Raquel at the crane.

Raquel brushed the dirt off the back of Marco's shirt. "I wonder who they're going to get to replace Miss Mac," she said.

"I don't know," Marco said. "Hope it's someone young."

Izzy chuckled. "Yeah. Miss Mac had to have been, what? A hundred?"

Marco nodded and smiled. His grin quickly faded. "That was pretty weird, wasn't it? I can't believe Miss Mac died right there in the classroom."

"I know," Raquel agreed. "That's got to be the scariest thing I've ever seen." She instinctively crossed herself.

Marco hopped up on one of the crane's wheels and sat down. "Man, she didn't deserve to die like that. She was a good teacher. After all the things she did for the school and everything, it seems that she should've been allowed to die at home, maybe over the Christmas break—or even during the summer. But not in the classroom with every-body laughing at her, thinking she'd fallen asleep."

The image of Miss Mac's lifeless body slumped in her chair had haunted Marco's dreams. He felt terrible for having joined in the laughter. He wished he had recog-nized that something was wrong with her. He would have run to the office and told someone instead of sitting there, giggling like an idiot.

"Well, like they say: 'When you gotta go, you gotta go,'" Izzy said, making light of the conversation. "I don't want to talk about Miss Mac's death. I feel bad about her dying and everything, but come on, she was *old*. That's what happens when you get old. I guess that means we won't have to turn in our book reports."

Their book reports were due that Friday, and Izzy still hadn't selected a book to read. He had planned on turn-ing in a book report he'd written the year before.

"Mine's done," Marco said. "I was going to turn it in the day she died."

"Yeah? What'd you read?" Izzy asked.

"*Fahrenheit 451* by Ray Bradbury."

"Never heard of it. Was it on the list?"

Marco climbed into the cab of the crane and sat in the driver's seat. He gripped the steering wheel and pretended to drive it. "No, but I asked Miss Mac if I could read it for my project, and she said it was okay. The title caught my attention when I saw it in the library."

"What's it about?" Raquel asked.

"It's about a time in the future when all books are banned. No one's allowed to read anything. Any books found are burned."

"Hey, now that's my kind of future," Izzy wisecracked. "No books and no book reports."

"Anyway, I'm holding on to my book report in case the new teacher asks for it."

"The new teacher," Izzy grumbled. "With my luck, she won't be a hundred years old. She'll probably be two hundred."

Raquel glanced at her watch. It was after five. "I have to go. My dad will be home soon, and I have to help my mom fix dinner."

They headed for the Santa Maria Apartments. When they arrived at Raquel's door, she gave Marco and Izzy a hug before going in.

CHAPTER SIX

Raquel's little brother Ignacio sat on the living room floor watching an episode of "The Simpsons." He was snacking on dry Cheerios from a bowl he held in his lap.

"Hi, Nachito, *¿dónde está Mami?*"

Ignacio looked up at his sister, grinned a mouthful of Cheerios, and pointed toward the back of the apartment.

As Raquel headed to the kitchen, she heard the sizzling sounds of something cooking.

Her mother stood at the stove, browning a clump of ground beef that would become *picadillo* after potato wedges, tomatoes, and spices were added to it.

"*Hola*, Mami." Raquel kissed her mother on the cheek.

"Wash your hands. Then get the beans out of the refrigerator," Raquel's mother told her in Spanish.

A portable black-and-white TV on the countertop was tuned to the evening news. While Raquel ran her hands under the water from the faucet, her eyes were drawn to it. It was airing a clip about the immigration protest rally that had been held in Dallas months earlier. Thousands of people, wearing white clothing, waving flags of the United States, Mexico, and other countries, had marched through the streets of Dallas, shouting phrases like "*¡Sí se puede!*"

A number of counter protestors had attended the rally, too.

"What is it about the word 'illegal' that you people don't understand?" an enraged fat woman on the news shouted at an old Mexican man.

The woman's voice made Raquel's skin crawl. If she had gone to the rally, she would've told her exactly what she thought the word "illegal" meant. But her parents refused to take her.

"It's too risky," her mother said. "We have too much to lose."

"We need to keep a low profile," her father added. "We don't need to bring any unnecessary attention to ourselves."

Raquel retrieved a Tupperware container from the refrigerator. She got a pan from a bottom cabinet under the stove and poured the container's contents into it. As she stirred the beans, she told her mother, "All we want is a better life. Papi works hard. So do you. Nachito and I make good grades in school. Since when is it illegal to want a better life?"

Her mother stirred the meat in slow, wavy motions. She did not answer. But her face had a troubled look.

After supper, Raquel went to her room. She pulled her diary from her nightstand and sat on her bed. She jotted down the day's events, including details of her time with Marco and Izzy at the construction site.

Then she scribbled the word "illegal."

That's what they said she was.

So were her mother and her father. And her little brother Ignacio. Criminals, too, according to some. The crazier ones even linked them to terrorists. She'd laugh if it wasn't for the fact that there were people who actually believed that garbage.

She thought back to the day when she and her family left Bustamante, Nuevo León, to come to the United States. Raquel was in the fourth grade. Her little brother was only three years old.

Raquel's father paid a *coyote* thousands of dollars, money he had saved up for years, to guide them across the border.

The *coyote* took them to Nuevo Laredo, Tamaulipas, a city that lies on the banks of the Rio Bravo, or what Americans call the Rio Grande River. The water in that part of the river was shallow, so they were able to wade across it without too much trouble.

All the while, they were on the constant lookout for the *Migra*, Border Patrol agents who drove their immigration vans up and down the dividing line between Mexico and the United States.

They hid among the giant reeds in the wetlands area, fearful of being caught and sent back.

Once they made it through the first checkpoint, the *coyote* took them to a small, white, wood-framed house. It belonged to the Garcías, friends of the *coyote*. Raquel and her family slept on the living room floor. They stayed at the house until the next evening when they took off again.

There was a second checkpoint they had to get past. Again they managed to elude the Border Patrol.

Raquel's father spoke a little English, enough to buy Greyhound bus tickets for his family. They traveled to San Antonio, where they met up with some people they knew from Bustamante. From there, they drove through various Texas cities, looking for work. Finally, Raquel's father found a job at the Maximum Motors Body Shop.

But after three years in the United States, they were still considered "illegal."

Raquel stared at the page and frowned. *What an ugly word*, she thought.

During supper, when the subject of the immigration rally came up, her father angrily said, "We didn't cross the border. The border crossed us. Texas was our land. *Era nuestra tierra.* It was the *americanos* who stole it from us. Illegally! If anybody is illegal, it's them."

Her mother nodded in agreement.

Raquel gazed down at the word "illegal." She finished her diary entry with *Yo no soy terrorista. Yo no soy criminal. ¡Y yo no soy* illegal!

CHAPTER SEVEN

"As you heard me announce over the P.A. this morning, the school board has granted us permission to name our auditorium in honor of Miss Mac," Mr. Rathburn told the TEAM 3 teachers during their weekly meeting.

The news was met with enthusiastic applause.

"We'll have to have a dedication ceremony," Mrs. Frymire said. "We'll invite students, parents, everybody."

"I'll take a look at the school calendar for a date when we can hold it," Mr. Rathburn said. "Then we can start working out the details."

He fished a glossy picture catalog out of his coat pocket and sat it on the table." I took the liberty of checking with a sign manufacturing company downtown for some ideas on what type of lettering we want on our auditorium."

The catalog was from a place called Signs of the Times. It contained photographs of company names and logos.

"These are three-dimensional letters that can go directly on the wall outside the school." Mr. Rathburn pointed to a picture of a white stone building with the name HASKELL & ASSOCIATES displayed across it in black letters. "We can also add lettering at the entrance of the auditorium inside the building. The backs of the letters light up, giving them a halo effect. They come in stainless steel, aluminum, brass, and acrylic."

"Brass lettering would be beautiful," Mrs. Frymire said. "And it would stand out nicely against the maroon walls of the auditorium."

Mr. Rathburn sighed. "The only problem is, we don't have the money in our budget to pay for it."

"How much money are we looking at?" Mr. Watts asked.

"A lot more than we've got, I'm afraid. Here's an estimate the company gave me for stainless steel." Mr. Rathburn produced an invoice sheet and passed it around. "Brass runs a little more."

When he read it, Mr. Watts widened his eyes and let out a soft whistle.

Mrs. Pruitt scanned the slip of paper over his shoulder. "Why can't the school district pay for the lettering? Isn't that their responsibility?"

"You would think so," Mr. Rathburn said. "But the only thing that was approved at the meeting was the naming of the auditorium. Any funds involved will have to come from us."

"Why don't we ask the PTA for the money?" Mr. Watts asked. "I think they'd be willing to cough up the bucks."

"I don't see why they wouldn't," Mrs. Frymire said. "They've certainly got the means. Besides, the parents loved Miss Mac. They'd do anything to keep her memory alive."

"I agree. I'll bring it up when we meet on Thursday." Mr. Rathburn collected the catalog and the invoice sheet. "By the way, Mrs. Frymire, have you had a chance to talk to your team about what you shared with me?"

"No, I wanted to wait until we were all together." Mrs. Frymire dug into her tote bag. She brought out a manila folder. "I discovered this while I was cleaning out Miss Mac's file cabinet."

"What is it?" Mr. Watts asked.

She opened the folder and revealed its contents—a rumpled bunch of papers stapled together. "It's a play Miss Mac wrote. *Thirteen Days to Glory — The Battle of the Alamo*," she said, reading the title on the front page. "I told Mr. Rathburn that I thought it would be a touching gesture if our seventh graders were to present Miss Mac's play in the auditorium once it has officially been named after her."

She passed the script around. The sheets were dingy and brittle.

Mr. Watts gingerly turned the pages. "When was this written? It looks ancient."

"I don't know. Miss Mac wrote lots of plays, but in the twenty-seven years I've been here, I can't recall ever seeing this one." Mrs. Frymire took back the script and asked, "What do you think?"

"I think we should do it," Mrs. Pruitt answered right away.

Mr. Watts gave her a skeptical look. "I don't want to douse the fire, Doris, but do any of us know anything about putting on a play? I mean, Miss Mac was the only talented one among us. We couldn't have done any of those shows without her."

Mrs. Frymire frowned. "Well, maybe we don't have Miss Mac's expertise, but I think we can pull it off. We owe it to her. Besides, we have her script. If we pick out the right kids and have them memorize their parts, I'm sure we can present an adequate show, if not necessarily a great one."

Mr. Watts still wasn't convinced. "Putting on a play is a heck of a lot more difficult than just having kids memorize lines, Doris. You know that. We'll need lights, music, costumes, and . . . and what about the Alamo itself? Who's going to build it?"

Mrs. Frymire stared at Mr. Rathburn.

He shook his head. "Don't look at me. Hammering nails into walls is about the extent of my carpentry skills."

"What if we painted a huge mural of the Alamo and stapled it to the back wall?" Mrs. Pruitt suggested. "We could ask Ms. Posey and her art students to help us."

"No," Mr. Watts said. "We'll need a fully functional structure, something that can be placed in front of the kids." A smile slowly spread across his face. He slapped his hand on the table. "I know who can build it for us! Billy Ray Cansler's father's a custom carpenter. He remodels homes and stuff. I'll bet building an Alamo would be easy for him to do."

Mrs. Pruitt frowned. "I don't know, Barry. If we were to ask Billy Ray's father to build it for us, you know what that would mean, don't you? We'd have to put Billy Ray in the play."

"No problemo," Mr. Watts said. "We'll stick him in the back. Some place where he can't cause too much damage."

Mrs. Frymire slipped the folder back into her tote bag. "We'll have to do better than that, I'm afraid. If we're going to ask his father to build the Alamo, he's going to expect his son to have a bigger role in the play than just being an extra in the background."

"Why don't we start with naming the auditorium after Miss Mac," Mr. Rathburn said, interrupting their discussion. "We can worry about the play later."

"That reminds me, have you heard anything about Miss Mac's replacement?" Mrs. Pruitt asked.

"No. Personnel's interviewing prospective candidates, that's all I know. We should hear something soon, though."

"Hopefully they'll send us someone who's also a custom carpenter," Mr. Watts muttered.

CHAPTER EIGHT

Izzy Peña was running for his life. He flew past the library, turned the corner, burst through the double doors of the school, and ran outside. If only he could find Marco.

Maybe I can lose them in the crowds.

Izzy was out of breath and full of fear.

He stopped momentarily and glanced over his shoulder. Billy Ray Cansler and Luther Bowers threw the doors open. The Bukowski twins, Jacob and Joshua, spilled out from the doors with them.

Izzy sped off again. He ran across the blacktop, zigzagged his way through a group of kids shooting baskets, and rounded the corner of the gym. Without slowing down, he looked back.

He was still being chased.

Not watching where he was going, he crashed into a couple of girls who were sharing a *People* magazine. One of the girls spun around and fell, landing on her backside. The other one tumbled forward, skinning her knee on the blacktop surface. She yelped an "Ow! Ow!" as she rolled over on her side, clutching her leg. Izzy saw a quarter-size red mark on the girl's knee where the flesh had been scraped off.

"I . . . I'm sorry," he stammered. "I . . . I didn't . . . "

But his attempt to apologize was interrupted. He saw Billy Ray and his gang plowing through the crowds. He had no choice but to leave the girls on the ground. Why hadn't he paid attention to where he was going? First it was Billy Ray. Now those girls.

Two minutes earlier, he had just paid for his breakfast. He was looking for a place to sit. That's when he saw Orlando Chávez, Felipe Garza, and some other guys sitting at a table by a window. Orlando was waving to him. He had saved a place for Izzy. Izzy waved back to acknowledge that he'd seen him. He smiled. He was going to be the envy of the table, no doubt about it.

Last night, he'd gone to the wrestling matches. Izzy was a huge wrestling fan. His Tío Beto bought the tickets as soon as it was announced that American Championship Wrestling was coming to town. Row seven! Too bad the matches wouldn't be shown on TV. Tío Beto explained that it was a "house show," not a televised event. Izzy had hoped to be on television. But it didn't matter. He'd gotten to see all the wrestlers in person. And the ACW heavyweight champion, the Angel of Death, had beaten Jumbo Jefferson in an incredible, "no-disqualification" match. Izzy couldn't wait to tell the guys all about it.

He was so absorbed in his thoughts about the matches that he didn't notice Billy Ray Cansler making an abrupt stop in front of him.

He walked right into Billy Ray, hitting him on the back with his tray. Izzy's plate skidded forward and slid off. The eggs and bacon spilled down Billy Ray's black, sagging pants. The carton of milk splashed on Billy Ray's black shirt.

Billy Ray loved to wear black. He thought black made him look cool. He also liked to sag his pants. He thought sagging his pants made him look tough. Only he didn't look cool or tough with eggs and bacon strips dangling from the waist of his pants and a big splotch of milk staining his shirt.

At that instant Izzy knew he was dead. He didn't even bother to say he was sorry. It'd just be a waste of time. He did the only thing he could do.

The best thing to do.

Run!

He circled the school and headed into the teachers' parking lot.

"I'm gonna getcha!" he heard Billy Ray holler.

Billy Ray and his gang were closing in.

Izzy slammed on the brakes just in time, avoiding his third collision of the morning.

A woman suddenly appeared in front of him. She had stepped out of a red convertible.

"Where's the fire?" she asked. "Or are you late for a hot date?"

She was young. Good-looking. Straight, shoulder-length, auburn hair and a warm smile with rows of perfect white teeth. Izzy thought she looked like a model, like one of those whose photos he sometimes saw in his mom's magazines. The woman had on a light-blue sweater with a picture of a glittery flying horse on the front.

Izzy gasped for air. "Some guys are chasing me!" He turned around and pointed.

"Who?" the woman asked, following his finger.

Izzy scanned the area, but Billy Ray and his gang had dissolved into the crowds. "They're gone." He inhaled and exhaled with short quick breaths.

"Why were they after you?"

Izzy hesitated. He wasn't sure he wanted to explain his situation to this woman. He didn't even know who she was. Anyway, what was it teachers were always preaching about—don't talk to strangers?

Izzy shrugged. "Just . . . because."

"Just because?" The woman flashed her toothpaste commercial smile. "Oh, I think there's a little more to your story than that." She waited for Izzy to answer. When it appeared that he wasn't going to volunteer any more information, she asked, "Can you show me where the main office is, then?"

"Yeah, sure." Izzy escorted her inside. Whoever this woman was, at least she'd be able to protect him from Billy Ray and his gang.

CHAPTER NINE

"Sandy Martínez, I'd like you to meet your new team." Mr. Rathburn directed her attention to the teachers sitting around the mahogany table in the conference room.

Mr. Watts was the first to stand. "Ms. Martínez, I'm Barry Watts." He stretched out his hand. "I'm the TEAM 3 seventh grade math teacher. Welcome to Rosemont."

She shook his hand. "A pleasure to meet you, Mr. Watts. And please, call me Sandy."

"Sandy it is," he said with a grin. "And I prefer to be called Barry." Mr. Watts could not believe his good fortune. Sandy Martínez was cute, a real welcomed addition to the team.

For the past six years he'd worked with the other women. Nothing wrong with that, he supposed. They were fine teachers — excellent, as a matter of fact. But they were all old enough to be his mother. Mrs. Pruitt, tall and thin, with tightly curled white hair that reminded him of a head of cauliflower, had a son who was two years older than he was. And Mrs. Frymire, a plump woman with a doughy face, claimed she was fifty-five years old. Maybe she was. But that big cloud of gray hair gave her the appearance of looking at least ten years older. Together with Miss Mac, the three of them made him feel like a caregiver at a retirement home. Yesiree, Sandy Martínez was definitely a nice change of scenery.

"Sandy? Claire Pruitt. I'm the Texas history teacher for our team. We're glad to have you."

"And I'm Doris Frymire. I teach science."

Ms. Martínez was a lot younger than Mrs. Frymire had expected. A lot prettier, too. She couldn't be any older than twenty-five, twenty-six tops. She wondered what kind of experience Ms. Martínez—Sandy—had to offer the team.

"Please sit down," Mr. Rathburn said.

Mr. Watts quickly pulled out a chair next to his. "Here you go."

Mr. Rathburn took his place at the head of the table. He folded his hands and leaned forward. "Ms. Martínez, I'm sure you're aware of the circumstances that led to your being sent to our school."

"Yes sir, I do."

"Miss Mac was an institution here. And I don't mind telling you, you have some mighty big shoes to fill."

Ms. Martínez straightened. "Mr. Rathburn, with all due respect, I'm not here to try to fill Miss McKeever's shoes. From what I've heard about her, I don't think anyone could. I do have my own style, though, my own approach to teaching. It may not be the Miss McKeever way, but I've been very successful in my career."

Feisty little thing, aren't you? Mrs. Pruitt thought.

"Yes, I know," Mr. Rathburn said. "You came highly recommended. What I meant to say was . . . " He paused. "Never mind. I'm sure you'll find your way around in no time."

"Pegasus," Mrs. Frymire muttered.

"I beg your pardon?"

"Pegasus," she repeated, pointing to Ms. Martínez's sweater. "And your earrings. They're flying horses, too."

"Oh. Yes." She touched her earrings. "You might say that Pegasus is my mascot."

"Your mascot?" Mr. Watts asked, bemused.

Ms. Martínez smiled. "I heard a story once, a long time ago, that gave me the idea to make Pegasus my mascot."

"Really?" Mr. Watts said with a bubbly look in his eyes. "You've got me curious, Sandy. Care to share the story?"

Ms. Martínez glanced at the others at the table. They looked back at her with expressions of indifference. Nevertheless, she leaned back in her chair and told her story.

"There once was a man who, because of his crimes, had been sentenced to death. He was taken before the king for the official pronouncement of his fate. There, the man fell to his knees and begged for his life. 'Please, Your Majesty,' he cried, 'let me live, and everything I have will be yours. Everything!'

"The king gazed down at the man and sneered at him. He asked, 'What can you possibly give me that I don't already have? I am the king! I have wealth. I have power. You have nothing to offer me.'

"With that, he turned and started to walk away. But the man called out, 'Your Majesty, let me go and . . . I will teach your horse . . . how to fly!'"

Ms. Martínez's voice grew louder, and her pace quickened as she told her story.

"Naturally, this stopped the king in his tracks. 'What did you say?' he asked.

"The man rose to his feet. 'It is true, O King. Set me free, and within a year, I promise you, I will teach your horse how to fly.'

"This was absurd, of course, and the king knew it. The man was simply saying this to save his life. On the other hand, the king thought, what if the man was telling the truth? What if somehow he actually had the ability to teach a horse how to fly? Now the king was right. He did possess untold wealth and power. But he did not own a horse that could fly. The more the king thought about it, the more he decided he had nothing to lose. So he told the man, 'All right, I will set you free. And I will give you a year. Within the year, you must teach my horse how to fly. If you cannot do it, then I will have you brought back here where you will be put to death immediately.'"

"Did the man teach the horse how to fly?" Mr. Watts asked. He loved the sound of her voice. It was like the song of an angel. He hoped she didn't have a boyfriend.

Ms. Martínez winked at him. "Let me finish my story and you'll find out."

Her playful wink made his heart race. He subtly inhaled the scent of her perfume. Roses. Her perfume smelled like roses.

Ms. Martínez continued. "As soon as he was released, the man raced out the palace doors. He was running down the steps when, by coincidence, he saw a friend coming up the stairs. The friend was shocked at seeing the man loose.

"'W . . . What are you doing out here?' he asked, frantically looking around. 'Did you escape?'

"The man calmly replied, 'No. The king set me free.'

"The friend was incredulous. 'Why would he do that? He was about to have you put to death. In fact, that's why I'm here. I wanted to see you once more before you died.'

"The man explained how he had promised the king that he could teach his horse how to fly within a year. That's why he had been released.

"'But that's impossible!' the friend exclaimed. 'You can't teach a horse how to fly.'

"The man smiled wryly and said, 'Maybe I can't. Then again, maybe I can. At any rate, I have a year. Lots of things can happen in a year. Within the year, the king might die. In which case, I have nothing to worry about. Or, his horse might die. If that happens, I will be free of my obligation. Or, I might die of natural causes rather than at the blade of the executioner's axe. Or, who knows? Maybe, within the year, I just might teach that horse how to fly!'"

Mrs. Frymire was confused. "That's an interesting story, Sandy, but what does it mean?"

"It doesn't have to mean anything, Doris," Mr. Watts said, coming to his new team member's defense. "It's only a story."

"Oh, it has special significance," Ms. Martínez said. "To me, anyway. You see, I think about that story at the beginning of each school year. I've discovered, as I'm sure you have, that teaching some of our kids may, at times, seem almost as impossible as trying to teach a horse how to fly. But . . . " She flashed a wide grin. "We do have a year. Lots of things can happen in a year. Each one of my students is going to be successful in my classroom." Her voice grew stronger. "And I will teach the horse how to fly!"

Mr. Watts stood and clapped. "Now that's what I call confidence."

Neither Mrs. Pruitt nor Mrs. Frymire seemed to share Mr. Watts's enthusiasm for their new teammate's story. They eyed each other knowingly.

I want to see her teach Billy Ray Cansler how to fly, Mrs. Pruitt thought.

Mrs. Frymire seemed to read her mind. *This young woman has lots to learn,* she thought back at her.

CHAPTER TEN

"Gotcha!"

Billy Ray shoved Izzy Peña from behind and slammed him against the lockers. He grabbed a fistful of Izzy's hair and yanked his head back. Luther and the Bukowski twins crowded around him to make sure he didn't escape.

"Ouch!" Izzy screamed.

"Where are your glasses, Izzy?" Billy Ray growled in his ear.

"P . . . Please. I . . . I'm sorry. I didn't mean . . ."

"Where are your glasses?"

"I . . . I don't wear g . . . glasses, Billy Ray."

Billy Ray pulled Izzy's hair tighter. Izzy felt as if his neck was going to snap in half. "Of course you don't, you pinhead! 'Cause if you did, then maybe you'd have seen where you were going!"

"I . . . I'm sorry," Izzy whimpered.

"Sorry? You're gonna be sorry all right!"

Billy Ray jerked Izzy's head back even harder. He was about to slam it into the lockers.

"Let him go!" a voice rang out.

Billy Ray turned.

Marco Díaz, flanked by Orlando Chávez and Felipe Garza, approached them.

"Stay out of this, Marco!" Billy Ray cried. "This is none of your business."

Marco crossed his arms and scowled. "You pick on my friends, and I make it my business." Orlando and Felipe nodded together.

Billy Ray loosened his grip. Izzy pulled away and scurried to Marco's side.

"Did you see what he did to my shirt?" Billy Ray turned and showed Marco his back. The milk had dried, but a stain resembling the map of Texas remained.

"Yeah. It was an accident. Izzy didn't do it on purpose."

"I don't care. He's gonna pay for this."

"Leave Izzy alone," Marco said in a calm but serious tone.

Billy Ray gazed up at him. With Luther and the Bukowski brothers standing beside him, he boldly declared, "I ain't scared of you, Marco."

"Leave Izzy alone," Marco repeated with that same calmness.

"You think you're tough, don't you?" Billy Ray scoffed. "Just 'cause you're a boxer. Well, I've beaten up guys a lot tougher than you with no problem."

"Leave . . . Izzy . . . alone."

"You looking for a fight?" Billy Ray spread out his arms to show he wasn't scared. "Is that what you want?"

He was bluffing. There was no way he would fight Marco Díaz. Not by himself, anyway. Marco was a boxer in the Golden Gloves. And Billy Ray was nobody's fool.

When he saw Izzy in the hall on the way to the gym, he thought he'd take care of him real quick. Show Izzy what it meant to cross paths with him. Now he had to contend with Marco. Orlando and Felipe were nobodies. He could handle them easily. Just like he'd almost done with Izzy. But no matter what he said, there was no way he could beat Marco Díaz. Still, he couldn't just back away and let everyone think he was scared. Luckily, he had Luther and the Bukowskis with him.

"There they are, Mr. Watts!"

Myra Coonrod charged down the hallway, her finger pointing like a one-way sign. Strands from her wiry blond hair had escaped from the scrunchie she used to tie her hair back. They hung down her face like pieces of twine. "See? I told you they were fighting!"

"What's going on?" Mr. Watts demanded to know.

Billy Ray dropped his arms. Neither of the boys answered.

"Well?"

"Nothing," Billy Ray mumbled.

Myra's mouth fell open. Her eyes widened in exaggerated disbelief. "They were getting ready to beat Izzy up!"

Mr. Watts turned to Izzy. "Is that true?"

Izzy stared at Billy Ray. Then he looked up at Mr. Watts. "No sir, nothing happened." Izzy didn't want to fuel the fire. As far as he was concerned, it was over. Hopefully. Anyway, he didn't want to look like a snitch in front of the guys.

"Are you sure?" Mr. Watts stared at Billy Ray and his gang with suspicion.

"We were just talking about stuff, sir," Billy Ray said innocently. "That's all."

Mr. Watts had no doubt that what Myra had reported to him was true, but with no one willing to admit to anything, there wasn't much he could do.

"I hope you boys are through *talking*," he said. "Because if you're not, then maybe I'll do some talking of

my own . . . first to Mr. Rathburn, then to your parents!
You get my drift? Now go on to P.E."

The boys dispersed in two groups. Billy Ray glowered
at Myra as he passed her. She stuck out her tongue at him.

"You go on, too, Myra," Mr. Watts said.

Myra stuck out her lower lip and blew the hair away
from her eyes. "But what about Billy Ray? Aren't you
going to do anything to him?"

"I did."

"But you should've seen what he was doing to poor
Izzy. He was really hurting him."

Myra didn't care about Izzy Peña. He didn't mean
anything to her. She hardly even talked to him. But she
was dying to get Billy Ray in trouble.

She hated Billy Ray. Ever since he laughed in her face
when she invited him to her birthday party, she'd wanted
to pay him back.

If only he knew how much courage it had taken her to
invite him in the first place. She was almost certain Billy
Ray would turn her down, but she decided to try anyway.

Billy Ray was one of the cool kids at school. If he went
to her party, then maybe some of the girls would think
she was cool, too.

"It's been taken care of, Myra," Mr. Watts said.

"But Billy Ray . . . "

Mr. Watts held a hand up to her face like a crossing
guard stopping traffic. "It's been taken care of, Myra," he
said again. "Now, go on."

Myra's shoulders slumped. "Aw, man." Reluctantly,
she trudged down the hall.

CHAPTER ELEVEN

After Myra disappeared through the doors of the gym, Mr. Watts decided to check on his new colleague.

Ms. Martínez was standing on an aluminum ladder. She had covered the rear wall of her classroom with blue butcher paper. On it she painted a large, winged horse flying across a clouded sky. She was stapling an arched caption above it in white letters that would read: ALWAYS AIM HIGH!

Mr. Watts stood at her doorway and observed her for a few seconds. "I see you've already begun teaching horses how to fly."

She flinched and spilled her letters.

"Sorry, I didn't mean to startle you." Mr. Watts rushed to the back of the room and gathered the letters for her. "Here you go."

"Hi, Barry. I didn't hear you come in." Ms. Martínez took the letters and added them to her display.

"You're a pretty good artist, you know that?"

"Thanks. Glad you like it." She stepped down from the ladder and put her stapler on her desk.

"Think you could paint a picture of the Alamo?"

"I don't know. I've never tried. Why?"

"I guess Doris hasn't told you yet."

"Told me what?"

Mr. Watts sat on top of a student desk. He pulled out a chair and propped his feet on it. Then he shared their plans with her.

"That is so sweet," Ms. Martínez told him. "Miss Mac must have been an awesome teacher. I wish I could've met her."

"Yeah, she was pretty cool for an old lady," Mr. Watts said. Then he frowned. "I was always a little scared of her, though."

Ms. Martínez grinned. "Scared? Why?"

"I don't know. I guess . . . I guess it was like having my grandmother hanging around all the time. I was always afraid of messing up in front of her and then getting scolded."

Ms. Martínez crossed her arms and studied his face. "Was she ever ugly to you?"

"No, but every once in a while, I'd say something she didn't like—something stupid. You know, just to be funny. She'd get real quiet. Then she'd give me *the look*." Mr. Watts raised an eyebrow and made a face.

Ms. Martínez smiled. "I know that look. My mom's a master at it. I think it's something people automatically acquire when they become senior citizens."

"That, and discount meals at Denny's," Mr. Watts joked.

She laughed affectionately.

Mr. Watts raised his eyebrow again. She tried to copy him, but her brows furrowed together, and her expression was more of pain rather than irritation.

"It takes practice." Mr. Watts raised his brow once more, then he bounced it up and down in rapid motions.

"When are you planning to present Miss Mac's play?" Ms. Martínez asked, giving her eyebrows a rest.

"We don't have a definite date yet, but since March is Texas History Month, we thought that'd be a good time. Also, I think Doris wants to wait until the auditorium has officially been named after Miss Mac."

"When will that happen?"

"I don't know. You'll have to talk to Doris. She's pretty much in charge of the whole shindig. Me? I just wait till I'm told what to do."

He climbed off the desk and gazed up at the large picture of The Cat in the Hat stapled on one of the walls. Next to it was a caption that read: THIS IS GOOD! THIS IS FUN! LOOK AT THE GREAT WORK 7th GRADE HAS DONE!

The black and white cat, with its oversized red and white top hat and red bowtie, was pointing to an empty space. The empty space, Mr. Watts presumed, would soon be the home of the "great work" the cat was proudly touting.

There was a knock at the door. Mrs. Pruitt and Mrs. Frymire entered.

"Hello, Ms. Mart . . . Sandy," Mrs. Frymire said. "We thought we'd stop by to see if you needed anything." Her eyes were drawn to the flying horse on the wall and the caption. They darted to the Cat in the Hat picture, then to the windows. The windows were decorated with blue balloon vallences. The vallences had pictures of white puffy clouds. They matched the backdrop of the flying horse.

This looks like a third-grade classroom, she thought.

"I was just telling Sandy all about Miss Mac's play," Mr. Watts said.

"It sounds great!" Ms. Martínez said. "When do you plan to start working on it?"

"Well, the dedication ceremony is a week from Monday," Mrs. Frymire said. "We could hold auditions the following Tuesday. Then I'd like for us to begin working on it right after that."

"I'll be more than happy to help with anything I can," Ms. Martínez offered.

"Thank you, Sandy," Mrs. Frymire said. "We'll send out permission slips before then, but we'll make an official announcement about the play at the ceremony. In the meantime, talk it up in your classes. I want as many kids as possible to get involved."

"We've already covered the unit on the Alamo in Texas history, but I'll go over the material again," Mrs. Pruitt added.

Mr. Watts clapped his hands. "All right. Now we're rocking."

CHAPTER TWELVE

Marco sat on a hill of gravel rocks at the construction site with Raquel and Izzy. About thirty feet away, they set up some Coke cans the workers had left strewn on the ground. Marco flung a large rock, striking one of the cans. The can wobbled back and forth like a drunk, but it didn't fall.

"What do you guys think of the new English teacher, Ms. Martínez?"

Raquel shrugged. "She's okay. A lot younger than Miss Mac, that's for sure. She's kind of pretty."

"Pretty?" Izzy fell back on the gravel hill. He spread out his arms as if he were making a snow angel. "Man, she is *hot!*"

Raquel stared indignantly at him. "She's old enough to be your mamá, *chiflado*."

A goofy smile spread across his face. "Yeah, my *mamacita!* When she talked to the class about the Alamo play this morning, I thought, sign me up. And I don't even like acting."

Marco scooped up a handful of rocks and sifted through them for the largest one. He chose a black one with white specks and flung it, knocking down one of the cans.

"I'd like to be in the program. Sounds like it's going to be a lot of fun. The Texans vs. the Mexicans, guns blazing, cannons firing, the whole works. But the Golden Gloves Tournament's coming up, and I've got to get ready for that." He turned to Raquel. "How about you? Are you going to try out?"

"No," she answered bluntly.

Izzy propped himself up on his elbows. "Why not?"

Raquel shook her head and muttered, "Not interested." She picked up a rock and threw it as hard as she could.

Clang!

She hit the middle can, sending it and the others scattering like pigeons.

"I'm sure there'll be lots of parts for girls," Izzy persisted. "Maybe you could be . . . "

Raquel whipped her head around and shot him an icy stare. "No!"

Izzy reeled back. He didn't know why she had answered so angrily, but he'd been around her long enough to know that when she got that tone in her voice, you didn't argue. To change the subject, he told Marco, "You take that boxing stuff pretty seriously, don't you?"

"Yeah, I guess. My grandpa thinks I'm going to be the middleweight champ some day."

Izzy nodded. "I wish I had the guts to get into boxing. I wouldn't mind it as long as I didn't have to get hit."

Marco punched him on the arm. "Well, you're going to get hit, Iz. That's what happens in boxing."

"Hey, watch it." Izzy pulled away and massaged his arm. "But you want to know what the best thing about being a Golden Gloves boxer is, Marco? It's that jerks like Billy Ray *Cancer* are scared of you. You're the toughest guy in the whole school. Everybody knows it, even Billy Ray."

"I don't know about that," Marco said, dismissing the compliment. "Anyway, that's not why I box. Sure, I want to know how to defend myself, but I really don't want to have to fight anybody, except in the ring." He rose and dusted off the back of his pants. "What you really need to do is stay away from Billy Ray. Then you won't have to worry about whether or not you can beat him in a fight. And you don't do yourself any favors by calling him names." He threw a rock, striking one of the fallen cans.

Izzy had a rock clenched in his hand ready to throw, but let it drop. "Are you telling me you don't think Billy Ray *Cancer* sounds funny? How about Billy Ray *Can't Learn*? That better?" He got up and brushed his pants. "Anyway, I didn't hit him with my tray on purpose. Like I told you guys, it was an accident."

Raquel looked at Izzy with concern. "Marco's right. Stay away from Billy Ray. Him and his gang. They're bad news."

"But I didn't even say anything to Billy Ray *Canker Sore*. That idiot's the one who stopped in front of me when he should've kept walking. It was his stupid fault, not mine. What do you . . . ?"

Something caught Izzy's attention. "Marco, Raquel, look," he whispered.

Near the fence, Blanca inched her way toward a white furry animal.

"That's the cabbit she was telling you about."

Marco glanced at the feline creature. Its ears were long and pointy. It looked like it was wearing a pair of snow-cone cups on its head. Its hair did seem to resemble rabbit fur. The animal was tailless; it only had a stump. A bunny tail, Blanca had called it. Still, Marco had his doubts. "Looks like a cat with long ears to me."

"I told you." Izzy picked up a rock. "Watch this."

Blanca stealthily crept up on her prey. She stretched out her hands.

Slowly.

Slowly.

Suddenly a large rock whizzed by her and struck the ground near the animal. Alarmed, the creature tore off and scrambled under the fence.

Blanca spun around. "Izzy! Why'd you do that? I almost had him."

Izzy laughed hysterically.

Raquel scowled at him. "Yeah, why'd you do that?"

Izzy stopped laughing. "Why are you taking her side? I was just having a little fun with her."

"Oh, Blanca's having a lot of fun, isn't she?" Raquel said sharply.

Blanca tried to suppress the tears that had begun to seep from her eyes. "Why do you always have to be so mean to me?"

"'Cause that's what little sisters are for," Izzy snickered. "I don't know why you're trying to catch that dumb cat, anyway. You know Mami's not going to let you keep it. Remember last year when she accidentally ran over Pulgas? She said we'd never have another pet."

"But this isn't a dog." Blanca stared at the wooden fence, hoping the animal would reappear. "It's a cabbit. And if I ever catch it, I know she'll let me keep him."

"It's just a long-eared cat," Izzy said, exasperated. "Even Marco said so. Didn't you, Marco?"

Marco glared at him. "I said he looked like a cat with long ears. But I could be wrong." He hoped Blanca would accept his explanation as an apology. He bent down and wiped a tear from her face. "I'll tell you what, Blanca. If I see the cabbit, I'll try to catch it for you, okay? I promise."

Izzy's sister smiled. "Thank you, Marco. And once you catch it, you'll see that it's not a regular cat."

"That's right," Izzy said with irritation in his voice. "And after you catch it, maybe you can go after a ca-dog, too. Or a ca-rat, or how about a ca-monkey?"

He walked away, mad that Marco was encouraging his sister. Worse, he was coming off as a hero, rescuing Blanca from her big bad brother. How come Marco had to be so nice all the time? Izzy liked it better when Marco faced down jerks like Billy Ray or the Bukowski brothers. Marco was tough. That was part of the reason he was friends with him. Izzy knew he could always count on Marco to protect him. But the way Marco acted toward Blanca. He treated her as if . . . as if she were his *own* sister.

Raquel, too, was encouraging her. Why were they playing along with Blanca? They both knew it was a cat.

He climbed up one of the girders of the building frame. "Hey, look up here," he shouted. "I think I just saw a ca-bird!"

CHAPTER THIRTEEN

The words, THE JOSEPHINE MCKEEVER MEMORI-AL AUDITORIUM, in bright, polished, brass letters, welcomed the invited guests. Every seat had long been filled. The latecomers had to settle for standing along the walls.

Mr. Jenkins, the scout master for Boy Scout Troop 232, opened the ceremony. He puffed out his chest like a rooster and marched to the front of the auditorium. "Ladies and gentlemen, please rise for the opening ceremonies!"

The packed house stood.

"Color Guard, advance!"

Andy LaFleur and Moe Craddock, dressed in their Boy Scout uniforms, entered in step, down the outside aisles, carrying the American and Texas flags. When they reached the front, they turned and walked toward each other.

"Color Guard, halt!"

Andy and Moe stopped. They turned to the audience and raised their flags high in the air.

"Please join us in the Pledge of Allegiance to the American and Texas flags." Mr. Jenkins snapped three fingers to his brows. Then he led the audience in both pledges.

After the flags were retired and everyone was seated, the seventh-grade choir performed "Journey's End," a song composed for the occasion by the choir teacher, Mr. Gewertz.

Karen Ingram, a student, read a poem she wrote titled "In Remembrance." It was followed by the Power Point presentation of Miss Mac's teaching career, which had been shown at her funeral.

Mr. Rathburn spoke. He began by acknowledging the PTA, thanking them for their generosity in paying for the lettering that spelled out Miss Mac's name, both on the outside and on the inside of the auditorium. At times his voice cracked as he shared his recollections of the much-beloved teacher. "Although I was her immediate supervisor, I often found myself turning to her for advice," he admitted as he closed his remarks. "She was truly *my* hero."

With that cue, Mr. Gewertz's choir sang "Wind Beneath My Wings."

Loud sniffles echoed throughout the auditorium as the choir crooned, "Did you ever know that you're my hero? You're everything I wish I could be . . . "

When the song was over, Mr. Rathburn directed the audience's attention to an easel standing on the right side of the podium. It was draped with a blue velvet cloth.

"This will hang in the foyer at the entrance of the auditorium," he told the audience, his eyes brimming with joy. Then, like a magician performing a magic trick, he pulled back the blue cloth, revealing a 24" x 30" portrait of Miss Mac. It was encased in an ornate gold frame. The audience responded with a rousing ovation.

Rose Adderly, Miss Mac's sister, addressed the crowd next. She expressed her deepest appreciation for the love the school and the community had shown toward her sister. "Right now, Josie's watching all of this from heaven, and knowing her, she's probably complaining to the angels about all the fuss being made over her," she joked. "But I want you to know that as much as you loved her, she loved you even more."

Finally, Mr. Rathburn announced that The Josephine McKeever Memorial Auditorium would soon host its first stage production. The seventh graders would present *Thirteen Days to Glory — The Battle of the Alamo*, an original play written by Miss Mac. This was met with thunderous applause.

When the ceremony was over, the TEAM 3 teachers caught up with Billy Ray Cansler's father.

"Sure, I can build an Alamo for you," Mr. Cansler said. "Not a problem. 'Course, I'm just talking about a façade, mind you. I ain't planning on building the real thing."

"No, of course not," Mrs. Frymire said.

"But I can add some steps on either side of the Alamo with a catwalk in between where the kiddos can stand."

"Sounds real enough to me," Mr. Watts said. "I'll be glad to help you in any way I can. I'm not much of a carpenter, but I can swing a pretty mean hammer." He pantomimed hammering a nail.

"Now, I'll build it for you, but I ain't no artist," Mr. Cansler told the group. "Someone else will have to paint it for you."

"Sandy can do it," Mr. Watts said. He turned to Ms. Martínez. "Can't you?"

She shrugged. "I guess I can." Then more confidently she said, "Sure. If Mr. Cansler will build the façade, it'll simply be another canvas for me to work on. I can even get some of the students to help."

"Good," Mr. Cansler said. "But, let's be clear on this. I'm only loaning you the materials. I want whatever's still usable back after you're through. You know, for my business."

"We understand," Mrs. Frymire said. "We won't have any use for the Alamo once we've done the show. Besides, we don't have any place to store it."

Mr. Cansler's voice softened. "I think what ya'll are doing for Miss Mac is a wonderful thing. She was a good teacher. Shoot, she was the only one who could keep Billy Ray in check," he added with a shameless grin. He surveyed the stage area, taking mental measurements. "I know my boy can be a handful at times. But I think being in this play will be good for him. We'll all look forward to seeing him up there."

He left after he saw his son and Joshua Bukowski trying to stomp on a kid's feet.

"Well, there you have it," Mrs. Pruitt said. "There's no way around it. We have to put Billy Ray in the play. That's probably the only reason his father's agreed to build the Alamo for us. And we won't be able to hide him in the back, either."

"I'm sure we can give Billy Ray a speaking part," Ms. Frymire said. "It's only fair if his father is going to do all that work for us. Besides, he may surprise us and do just fine."

"I just hope he doesn't end up ruining the show," Mr. Watts murmured.

Ms. Martínez turned to Mrs. Frymire. "I have a concern about the play. According to the script, Susanna Dickenson is the only female character in it. We don't have anything else for the girls to do."

Mrs. Frymire smiled. "I've already thought about that. I spoke to Jay Gewertz and asked him if he would teach the kids Texas songs. The girls can make up most of the choir."

"We can also use girls to serve as the narrators," Mrs. Pruitt said.

Ms. Martínez nodded. Then an idea struck her. "You know, I could also teach a dance or two to add to the program."

Mrs. Pruitt looked at her warily. "What kind of dances are you talking about?" She envisioned Ms. Martínez teaching the kids some of those "hip-hop" things she sometimes caught on TV while she channel-surfed.

"I was thinking about square dances. I have a copy of 'Cotton-Eyed Joe' as well as some other songs we might be able to use."

"That'll be all right, I suppose," Mrs. Pruitt said with doubt in her voice. She was not impressed by Sandy Martínez's eagerness to become involved with the play. She'd never even met Miss Mac.

"You betcha," Mr. Watts said. "This sounds like it's going to be a terrific show. I can hardly wait to get started."

CHAPTER FOURTEEN

On Tuesday after school, over a hundred chatty, noisy, seventh graders gathered in The Josephine McKeever Memorial Auditorium for the Alamo tryouts.

Marco still hadn't decided about being in the program. He needed to find out if rehearsals would interfere with his training.

Agatha Hornbuckle was there to audition for the role of Susanna Dickenson, the heroic survivor of the Alamo. Her sister Brenda had played Titania in the previous year's production of *A Midsummer Night's Dream*. Agatha had to endure listening to her mother prattle on about what a great actress Brenda was. How she had memorized pages and pages of dialogue in such a short time. Agatha would show her mom, her sister, everybody, that she, too, could act.

When Mrs. Frymire announced that Susanna Dickenson was the only female character with a speaking part in the play, Agatha knew she had to have that role.

She pulled out her compact from her purse and gazed at her reflection in the mirror. She made a face when she saw that the pimple on her forehead was still there, protruding, she thought, like a third eye. The concealer her mother had given her to apply on it only partially hid the ugly growth. Agatha smoothed her bangs over it and hoped she could keep it hidden. She took out a tube of lipstick and recolored her lips. COTTON CANDY PINK, the label on the lipstick tube read.

Mrs. Frymire stood center stage in front of the podium. "Let me have your attention!" she spoke into the microphone.

The chattering continued.

"Let me have your attention!"

The voices grew louder.

Mrs. Pruitt jumped up from her seat. "Hush!" she yelled. "You kids are getting out of control!"

More talking.

Ms. Martínez climbed up on the stage. She walked toward Mrs. Frymire. "May I?" She took the microphone from her hand. "Ring! Ring!" she said in a singsong voice. "Ring! Ring!" she repeated.

The kids stopped talking. "Hello?" they answered in unison.

They learned this routine on their first day in her classroom. It was Ms. Martínez's way of getting their attention.

"*Buenas tardes,*" she warmly greeted them.

"*Buenas tardes,*" they echoed.

Mrs. Frymire's lips tightened. She shot Ms. Martínez a disapproving glare. *Who does this little girl think she is? I can handle the kids just fine. I don't need her help.*

Ms. Martínez pointed at her T-shirt. On it was a picture of the Cowardly Lion from *The Wizard of Oz.* "Can anyone tell me who this is?"

"Mr. Rathburn?" Billy Ray Cansler cried out.

The crowd laughed.

Ms. Martínez's short years of experience as a middle school teacher had already taught her not to become easily fazed by sarcastic comments from troublemakers. She glanced down at the picture of the Cowardly Lion.

"Well, what do you know? He does sort of resemble our esteemed principal."

The crowd laughed again.

"Actually, the reason I wore this shirt today is because, in an odd way, it sort of reminds me of the story of the Alamo. Of the brave men, on both sides, who fought for what they each believed was right, displaying an incredible amount of courage. Which, as you all know, was the main thing this guy was lacking." She jabbed a thumb at the Cowardly Lion's face.

"That, and good looks," Agatha Hornbuckle said.

Ms. Martínez grinned. "You've got a point there, Agatha. I certainly wouldn't want him for a boyfriend. Wait a minute! I think I *did* date him. Once."

Myra Coonrod's hand shot up. "Ms. Martínez! Ms. Martínez! I have the DVD of *The Wizard of Oz*. I can bring it to school if you want me to."

Ms. Martínez had also learned not to become easily fazed by clueless kids. She smiled appreciatively. "Thank you, Myra. I'll let you know if we need it."

"I also have the sequel, *Return to Oz*," Myra said. "Only it's not really a sequel. I mean, it's not a musical like the first one, but I can bring that one, too, if you'd like."

Ms. Martínez winked. "Thank you, Myra. I'll keep it in mind."

She stepped away from the podium, smiled, and pointed to the audience with an outstretched hand. She told Mrs. Frymire, "It's all yours."

Mrs. Frymire glared at her. "Thank you," she said coldly.

Then she opened a black binder and put it on the podium. "First of all, I want to thank all of you for wanting to take part in our play, *Thirteen Days to Glory – The Battle of the Alamo*. This afternoon, we will hold auditions for speaking parts. But there will also be a choir, plus a couple of dances you can be involved in, if you choose. In addition, we will need lots of boys to play soldiers. If you are not selected for a speaking part, I hope you will consider participating as a singer, a dancer, or a soldier."

Myra Coonrod raised her hand. "Can girls be soldiers?"

"No, Myra. Boys only. Sorry."

"But that's sex discrimination!" Myra protested.

"You're very welcome to be in the choir if you'd like, Myra. Or in a dance."

"Why can't I be a soldier?"

"Because you fight like a girl, that's why!" Luther Bowers hollered.

"Shut up!" Myra stuck her tongue out at him.

Orlando Chávez asked, "Can we use fake blood in the play? I still have an almost full bottle of it left over from Halloween when I dressed up as Dracula. We could smear it all over our faces and on our clothes when we get shot. It washes off pretty easy."

"See, Mrs. Frymire?" Myra said. "That's why I want to be a soldier."

"No, Orlando, we are not going to use fake blood in the play. And I'm sorry, Myra, but you cannot be a soldier."

"Aw, man."

"How many boy speaking parts are there?" Andy LaFleur wanted to know.

Mrs. Frymire glanced down at her notes. "We have twelve speaking parts on the Texans' side, plus three other male speaking parts for Mexican Number One, Mexican Number Two, and Mexican Number Three."

Izzy Peña stood up. "I want to play Mexican Number One. 'Cause I'm the Number One Mexican!" He pointed proudly to his chest.

"Sit down!" Billy Ray yelled. "You're the Number One Mexican, all right. The Number One Mexican idiot!"

Marco Díaz wheeled around.

"Oops, sorry," Billy Ray snickered. "I didn't know your girlfriend was with you."

Mrs. Frymire read through her notes. "We'll also have six narrators, and I would prefer that they be girls."

"That's sex discrimination!" Luther Bowers shouted in a high voice, imitating Myra Coonrod.

Mrs. Frymire ignored him. "There's also one female character with a speaking part. Susanna Dickenson."

Agatha Hornbuckle waved her hand wildly in the air. "Ooh! Ooh! I want that one!"

Mrs. Pruitt craned her head and scowled at her.

Agatha dropped her hand and sank in her seat. "Sorry." Then she sat up. She clasped her hands together like she was praying. She looked up at Mrs. Frymire and mouthed the words: "Please, pick me! Please! Please! Please!"

Mrs. Frymire smiled at her, then looked away.

Allen Gray asked, "What about costumes? What are we going to wear?"

"Thank you for bringing that up, Allen," Mrs. Frymire said. "I would like for most of you to wear western clothing. You know, jeans, western shirts, cowboy hats, that sort of thing. But we'll need uniforms for the Mexican army. Do any of your parents sew?"

Izzy's hand went up. "My mom sews. She can sew anything."

"Then maybe we can get her to sew your mouth shut!" Billy Ray taunted.

"Billy Ray!" Mrs. Frymire cried. "Try to conduct yourself in an appropriate manner." Then to Izzy, she said, "I'll call your mom and ask her."

She explained the process for the auditions. She also placed a sign-up sheet on a table for those who wanted to be involved in nonspeaking roles.

The students were separated, boys on the left and girls on the right.

Karen Ingram was the first to read. She climbed up onstage where she was handed a sheet from the script.

"Start at the top and read the part of Narrator Number One," Mrs. Frymire told her.

Karen read: "In 1836, Texas was part of Mexico. Large numbers of American settlers moved there in search of a new life. These Texans, as they called themselves, agreed to accept and obey the laws of Mexico, and most of them even learned to speak Spanish in an effort to live in harmony with the Mexican people."

While Karen read, Raquel Flores slipped into the auditorium through the rear doors. She motioned for Marco to scoot over, then sat next to him.

Marco was surprised to see her. "You change your mind?"

Raquel narrowed her eyes. "No." Then she gave him a half smile. "I thought I'd come by and throw tomatoes at you and Izzy while you're up there."

Marco didn't understand why Raquel was so adamant about not being in the play. He wanted to ask her, but after the way she snapped at Izzy, he decided against it. Maybe she just didn't like being onstage. Somehow, though, he didn't think that was it.

When Karen finished, Mrs. Frymire said, "Good job. You read with lots of expression."

Arlene Furr read next, followed by Judy Welch, Norma Herrera, Sylvia Gonzales, and Alma Crowthers.

When it was Agatha Hornbuckle's turn, she told Mrs. Frymire, "I'm here to audition for the part of Susanna Dickenson."

Mrs. Frymire smiled. "I understand, Agatha, but right now, all I want to do is hear you read. Once we've made a decision as to which students are selected for speaking parts, we'll assign specific roles. But I will take your request into consideration."

Agatha hesitated. She started to protest, but changed her mind. Finally she took the sheet of paper from the teacher and stood in front of the microphone.

"Read with expression," Mrs. Frymire encouraged.

Agatha straightened her skirt. She rubbed her lips together to even out her lipstick. She brushed her bangs over her forehead with her fingers.

"A . . . doctor . . . "

"A dictator," Mrs. Frymire corrected her.

"A dictator named An-Anto-ni-o López de Santa Anna threw out the Mexican Continue of 1824."

"That's 'Constitution,'" Mrs. Frymire said.

"Oh, sorry. The Constitution of 1824."

Raquel laughed. "I don't know why Mrs. Frymire's letting Agatha try out," she told Marco. "Everybody knows Agatha can't read."

"Then why don't you get up there and show her how it's done," Marco teased.

Raquel crossed her arms and faced the front. "No, thanks."

"He deneed . . . "

". . . denied."

". . . denied all citizens their rights and freedoms guaran-ted . . . "

". . . guaranteed."

". . . guaranteed under the . . . competition."

"Constitution."

"Constitution."

"Thank you, Agatha," Mrs. Frymire said. "You may step down."

"But I'm not through reading."

"That's all right. Good try, though."

Agatha's face twisted in anguish. "Mrs. Frymire, I'm sorry I messed up a little bit, but that's only because what I really want is to audition for Susanna Dickenson. Could I please read that part?"

"I'm sorry, Agatha, but we still have lots of kids we need to hear."

"Please?"

Mrs. Frymire stared at her without responding.

Agatha's chin sank into her chest. She shook her head and sullenly walked off the stage.

Raquel rose from her seat. "See you boys later."

"Where are you going?" Marco asked.

"*Al baño.* I have to go wee-wee. I'll be back," she added in a deep, Arnold Schwarzenegger-Terminator voice.

Noticing her standing, Mrs. Frymire asked, "Raquel, would you like to read for us?"

She waved her off. "No, thank you."

Ms. Martínez stood up and faced her. "Are you sure, Raquel? You do such a wonderful job in my class." Ms. Martínez had been impressed that even though English was Raquel's second language, she spoke it better than many of her students who were born in the United States. "Come up here," she urged. "You're a good reader. Let's see what you can do."

Raquel had no intention of being in the program. Still, Ms. Martínez had asked. She liked her. She was so different from Miss Mac. Younger, prettier, much easier to talk to.

Raquel ambled down the aisle.

Mrs. Frymire handed her the script. "Read the part Agatha just read."

Raquel glanced over the page. Then she read: "A dictator named Antonio López de Santa Anna threw out the Mexican Constitution of 1824. He denied all citizens their rights and freedoms guaranteed under the Constitution. The Texans protested, but their concerns were ignored. Many Tejanos, Mexican natives living in Texas, wanted the Constitution of 1824 restored. However, most Texans began to realize that they would not settle for anything less than complete independence from Mexico, and they were willing to fight, and die, if necessary, to gain that freedom."

She read with clarity and eloquence. She paused between sentences for effect. She made a strong effort, as she always did whenever she read aloud, to conceal her accent.

"Wonderful, Raquel!" Ms. Martínez said. "You read it perfectly."

Raquel beamed.

"We need good readers for the play," Mrs. Frymire told her. "I'll certainly keep you in mind."

When she returned to her seat, Marco said, "You did pretty good up there. You sounded like a real *gringa*."

Raquel nodded, although she didn't like the "*gringa*" reference. *Maybe this won't be so bad,* she thought. She quickly blocked out that idea from her mind. She'd never allow herself to be in the program, even if it meant letting her teachers down.

She could never be in a show that made heroes out of people who stole her land.

CHAPTER FIFTEEN

Mrs. Frymire called several boys to read together. Moe Craddock, Andy LaFleur, and Marco Díaz were selected to read first.

Andy: "Colonel! Someone's coming! Halt! Who goes there?"

Moe: "Put that peashooter away before ya hurt yourself, sonny. I'm looking for William Travis."

Marco: "I'm Travis. And you must be Davy Crockett."

Andy: "*The* Davy Crockett? The famous Indian and bear fighter from Tennessee?"

Moe: "Well, I don't know about the famous part, and I never much cared for fightin' Injuns, but I just love scrappin' with them b'ars. Why, I'll have ya know that with Ol' Betsy here, I once killed forty-seven b'ars with forty-six shots."

Andy: "Forty-seven bears with forty-six shots? How was that possible, sir?"

Moe: "Well, two of 'em was dancin' the Cucaracha at the time."

Marco: "Crockett, you've got to be the biggest natural-born liar to come out of Tennessee. But you're also the toughest fighting man I know. Welcome to the Alamo."

Ms. Martínez leaned over and whispered to Mr. Watts, "They're all such good actors."

"Yeah. And I love the way Moe Craddock added that thick, country accent. I definitely want him to play Davy Crockett."

Billy Ray Cansler, Herb Williams, and Allen Gray read next.

When they were through, Mrs. Frymire called Izzy Peña, Orlando Chávez, and Felipe Garza to the stage. "Izzy, I want you to read the part of Mexican Number One."

"Yes!" Izzy cried.

"And Felipe, you'll be Mexican Number Two. Orlando, you're Mexican Number Three."

Izzy glanced over his part. Then he frowned. "Mrs. Frymire, do I really have to read it like this?"

She cleared her throat. "Yes."

Izzy shrugged. "Oka-ay." Then he read: "Jew are hereby ordered to leef dees meeshun at once. Eef dees order ees not obeyed, we weel deestroy de Alamo and all off de occupants een eet."

Raquel laughed out loud and clapped her hands. She wished she'd brought tomatoes. She'd throw one right now.

"I knew you were the Number One Mexican idiot," Billy Ray jeered from the audience. "Now you sound like it."

Mrs. Pruitt whirled around and gave him a dirty look. "That is unacceptable, Billy Ray!"

"Yeah, you buck-tooth, bald-headed orangutan!" Izzy chimed in. "That is unacceptable!"

"Izzy!"

"Well, he started it!"

Izzy didn't know why he called Billy Ray a buck-tooth, bald-headed orangutan. It didn't even make any sense. But it sure sounded funny. His classmates thought so, too. They hooted with laughter.

Billy Ray hopped out of his seat and spread his arms. "Come on down here and say that to my face, punk."

Mr. Watts stood up. "Billy Ray, we've already heard you read. You may leave now."

Billy Ray remained standing, glaring at Izzy.

Izzy wasn't worried. Marco was with him. Billy Ray wouldn't dare try anything as long as Marco was around.

"Come on, let's go," Mr. Watts ordered, pointing to the rear doors.

Billy Ray slipped out of his row, followed by Luther Bowers and the Bukowski twins. When he reached the top of the aisle, he shot Izzy the finger before leaving.

Orlando was called on to read next. "De time has come. We weel make plans to attack de Alamo for de las' time."

"Your part's as bad as mine," Izzy complained.

"You think that's bad?" Felipe said. "Listen to this: Pardon me, bot woodent eet be better to wait onteel Gómez arrives weeth de beeg cannons?"

Raquel winced. She had laughed at first, but she didn't find it funny anymore. Were they supposed to be playing soldiers? Or characters from a "Speedy Gonzalez" cartoon show? What were they going to do next? Put on big sombreros and run around the stage shouting *Arriba! Arriba!*

"Mrs. Frymire, these lines sound dumb," Izzy said. "Why do we have to read them like this?"

"Because that's the way the play was written," Mrs. Frymire replied without elaborating.

After everyone had tried out, Mrs. Frymire announced to the group that a decision would be made in the next couple of days about the speaking parts, and she would notify them of it during class.

As the students exited the auditorium, Marco caught up with Raquel. "I hope you change your mind about being in the program. You'll do a great job."

She furrowed her brows. "Gracias, meester. I'm hoppy jew tink so, bot I weel not be een eet," she answered mockingly before she walked out.

CHAPTER SIXTEEN

"That's what she told them, Doris. Can you believe it? Now I've got a bunch of kids questioning my knowledge, my expertise. I'm telling you, she needs to stick to her subject and leave the teaching of Texas history to me." Mrs. Pruitt's face was pinched tight. Her pale cheeks had developed a purplish hue.

"I agree," Mrs. Frymire said. "And did you see what she did to me onstage? She practically shoved me out of the way to get on the microphone. As if after twenty-seven years of teaching, I don't know how to settle kids down." She poured herself another cup of coffee. Mrs. Frymire kept a coffeemaker in her room. Every morning before school, she, Mrs. Pruitt, and Miss Mac had shared a cup of coffee before the students arrived. Though Miss Mac was no longer part of their morning breakfasts, Mrs. Frymire still made a full pot of coffee. Out of habit.

Mrs. Pruitt peered into the box of donuts and selected a chocolate one with sprinkles. "I really hate to confront her, Doris. You know me. I don't like confrontations. If there's one thing I don't like, it's confrontations."

"It's for her best, Claire. She's young and inexperienced. She's going to make mistakes. Sometimes, it's necessary to admonish a colleague."

Mrs. Pruitt bit into her donut. Some of the sprinkles flaked off and stuck to her chin. "I'll talk to her after school. But I want you to be there as a witness. I don't want this to turn into . . ."

There was a light tap on the frame of the open door.

"Good morning, ladies." Ms. Martínez stepped inside. "I hate to disturb your breakfast, but I wanted to take a look at the list of students you selected for speaking parts in the play."

Mrs. Frymire eyed Mrs. Pruitt. "Of course." She picked up the sheet of paper from her desk and handed it to her.

Ms. Martínez smiled when she saw the first name on it. "Moe Craddock will be the perfect Davy Crockett. Barry and I were hoping you'd choose him."

"Thank you. I'll speak to his mom about buying him a coonskin cap," Mrs. Frymire said. "Maybe she can also find a fringed jacket for him to wear."

Ms. Martínez frowned as her eyes moved down the list. "Billy Ray Cansler as William B. Travis? I thought we agreed Marco Díaz would get that part."

"No," Mrs. Frymire said. "We agreed to let him read for it, but I think Billy Ray will do a much better job than Marco. We picked Marco to play Jim Bowie. That's almost as big a role as Travis."

"But Billy Ray's so unpredictable," Ms. Martínez said. "We all know that. If he doesn't show up on the evening of the performance, the whole program could be ruined."

"Oh, he'll be there," Mrs. Pruitt assured her. "Didn't you hear his father the other night? Billy Ray's whole family will show up, I promise you. And I don't think they'll be happy having him stand in the background without a speaking part. Not after we've asked his father to build the Alamo for us."

"Well, what about giving him a smaller part, like Captain George Kimball?"

Mrs. Pruitt snorted. "George Kimball? Kimball only has one line toward the end of the play."

"I know. It's just that Travis appears in just about every scene," Ms. Martínez said, not at all happy with their decision.

Mrs. Frymire took her by the hand. In a motherly fashion, she said, "Sandy, let me give you a piece of advice from an old veteran. There are times when we have to do things we don't necessarily agree with. Things that might not seem right or just. But we do them for the greater good. And if Billy Ray's father is building the Alamo for us, like it or not, we owe it to him to give his son . . . "

"Preferential treatment?"

Mrs. Frymire smiled ruefully. "Let's just say that this is our way of compensating his father for what he's doing for us."

Ms. Martínez shrugged. "If that's how you feel about it." She read the next name. "Agatha Hornbuckle as Susanna Dickenson?"

Mrs. Pruitt straightened. "What's wrong with Agatha Hornbuckle?"

Ms. Martínez looked at her in disbelief. She felt as if she was on the receiving end of a practical joke. "Well, for starters, Agatha can't read."

Mrs. Frymire shut the donut box. For a second, she thought about offering Sandy a donut but changed her mind. "Well, I agree that Agatha's probably not the best reader in the seventh grade. But she has a certain stage presence. Besides, she won't be reading anything. She'll memorize her part."

"What about Raquel Flores? She was very good."

"So was Agatha," Mrs. Frymire replied adamantly.

Ms. Martínez sat the paper back on the desk. The list was not the real reason she had come to talk to her colleagues. She was stalling, trying to muster up the nerve to tell them what was really on her mind. She had already shared her concern with Mr. Watts. He said he understood but discouraged her from speaking out.

"Don't do it, Sandy. Please. You have to understand how things work around here. Leave it alone. Don't say anything. Just go along with it, okay?"

But she couldn't just go along with it. She had to say something.

"Mrs. Frymire, I realize Miss Mac was an icon here, a legend in her own time, if you will. From everything I've heard about her, she was an exceptional English teacher. Not only that, I also know she wrote and directed countless plays—plays people still rave about."

"That's right, she did," Mrs. Frymire said. Mrs. Pruitt nodded.

Ms. Martínez picked up the copy of the play sitting on Mrs. Frymire's desk. She took a deep breath. "But this one, *Thirteen Days to Glory – The Battle of the Alamo*, this one is . . . how shall I put it?" She probed her mind for the right words.

Mrs. Pruitt made a face. "What's wrong with it?"

Ms. Martínez licked her drying lips. "Don't get me wrong. I . . . I think most of the play is well written. Miss Mac must have done a lot of research before she wrote it. But . . . " She scrunched up her face. "But the dialogue for the Mexicans is . . . it's kind of offensive, don't you think?" Her voice climbed up in pitch.

Mrs. Pruitt's jaw tightened. "What do you mean?"

"Listen to this." Ms. Martínez flipped through the pages. *"Jew are hereby ordered to leef dees meeshun at once. Eef dees order ees not obeyed, we weel deestroy de Alamo and all off de occupants een eet."* She looked at her coworkers glumly. "Why did Miss Mac write the Mexican soldiers' parts with such an exaggerated accent?"

Mrs. Frymire shrugged. "Probably to make the characters sound more authentic. You know, to sound . . . *Mexicanish.*"

"Really?" Ms. Martínez raised an eyebrow in a questioning slant. *The look.* "Is that what you think I sound like?"

Mrs. Pruitt glared at her. "Don't try to turn this into a racial issue, Sandy, because it's not."

"I'm not trying to turn it into anything." Ms. Martínez swallowed dryly. "But the play's liable to offend every Latino in the audience, not to mention anyone else with a trace of sensitivity to the Mexican culture."

"Well, we'll just have to take that chance, Sandy." Mrs. Frymire assumed a posture of superiority. "Let me explain something to you. This play is a tribute to a great woman. And a great friend. Miss Mac dedicated her life to this school and its children. So, yes, we are going to present her play exactly as she wrote it."

Mrs. Pruitt sat her unfinished donut on a student table. She circled around Ms. Martínez and pointed a finger with a long red nail at her. "And as long as we're on the subject of the Alamo, there's something I want to ask you, Sandy. Some of the kids have been telling me that you said the Texas history book has it all wrong. That Davy Crockett gave up at the Alamo. That he surrendered. That he didn't die fighting. Is that true?" Her voice grew louder as she spoke.

Ms. Martínez was beginning to feel as if she had walked into an ambush. "I . . . I didn't tell them the book was wrong. I was only offering the kids another perspective of the Alamo story. Look, if you've read the José Enrique de la Peña account of what happened, you would know that in all probability Davy Crockett did surrender."

Mrs. Pruitt's upper lip began to twitch. "Did you also tell the kids that Travis didn't draw the line on the ground when he asked his men if they wanted to stay and fight, to cross it and join him?"

Ms. Martínez forced a smile. "Mrs. Pruitt, there are lots of myths about the Alamo story. That happens to be one of them."

"Oh, really? Well, then tell me this, Sandy. What makes you such an authority on the Alamo song?"

Ms. Martínez's heartbeat quickened. She did not want any trouble from them. This was her first teaching job after taking a leave of absence to finish up her master's degree. She wanted to get along with her coworkers even if she didn't agree with everything they said or did. "I . . . I grew up in San Antonio," she stammered. "Every year, we went on a field trip to the Alamo. I happen to love Texas history. But I don't claim to be an expert on it."

The veins on Mrs. Pruitt's skinny neck stood out in livid ridges. "Then do me a favor, Sandy, would you? Do you think you could do me one simple favor? Do you? Do you?" Flakes of donut mixed with spit flew out of her mouth. "Stick to your subject and leave the teaching of Texas history to me!"

Ms. Martínez jumped back, startled by Mrs. Pruitt's anger. "I . . . I'm sorry. I didn't mean any offense. E . . . Excuse me."

She dashed out the door just as the bell rang.

CHAPTER SEVENTEEN

Marco had one arm behind his back and a silly grin on his face. He walked up to Raquel, who was at her desk clearing out her backpack.

"Happy Valentine's Day!" He brought out a stuffed, black teddy bear and sat it in front of her.

Raquel sprang back and an involuntary "oh" escaped from her throat. For a second she thought Marco had dropped a cat on her desk.

"Like it?"

The bear was covered in coarse, bristly, black fur. It had a red, valentine-shaped nose. The inside of its ears and paws were lined with red felt. The bear held a huge red valentine with the words: "Be Mine, Valentine!" written in bold black letters.

Ugh, Raquel thought, but out loud she said, "Thank you, Marco. Happy Valentine's Day to you, too." She stood and gave him a hug.

"Watch this." Marco picked up the bear and squeezed its stomach. The bear spoke in a high, mechanical voice. It said: "I-love-you-more-than-honey."

He squeezed it again. This time it said: "You're-bear-y-spe-cial."

"Pretty cool, huh?"

Raquel had to clamp her lips shut for a few seconds out of fear that an unappreciated laugh would slip out. The bear reminded her of an old "Twilight Zone" episode she'd seen about a murderous talking doll. She was flattered that Marco had been thoughtful enough to buy her a Valentine's Day present. Maybe something could develop between the two of them after all. But if it did, one thing Marco was going to have to learn about her was that she hated stuffed animals, especially bears.

When Raquel was little, her Tía Chavela gave her a stuffed panda for her birthday. She'd bought it at the Chapultepec Zoo in Mexico City. But the *osito panda* gave Raquel the creeps. Its large round eyes scared her. They seemed evil, somehow. Every night before she went to bed, Raquel would turn the panda around to face the wall. She couldn't stand to have those big black eyes look at her. She gazed at Marco's Valentine teddy bear. It had those same spooky eyes.

As soon as the tardy bell rang, Mrs. Pruitt took attendance. Then she continued her Texas history lesson from the day before.

"After receiving word from James Bonham that no help would be coming, Colonel Travis ordered all the Texans, except the guards, to gather in the courtyard," she explained to her class. She was trying to undo the damage she felt Ms. Martínez had caused. "Jim Bowie, who had become ill during the siege, could no longer walk. He had to have some of the men carry him to the courtyard on a cot."

Marco raised his hand. "What was wrong with Bowie, Mrs. Pruitt?" He'd developed a special interest in him ever since he learned he'd been chosen to play Jim Bowie in the play. The part was perfect for him, he thought. Bowie was a tough guy, a fighter, a brawler. He might even have been a boxer if they'd had boxing back then.

"Tuberculosis, pneumonia, maybe a combination of the two," Mrs. Pruitt said.

Marco nodded. This was good information. It gave him an idea. Maybe he'd cough every once in a while as he delivered his lines to add realism to his character. He might also walk around with his shoulders slumped to show that he didn't feel well.

Continuing in a somber tone, Mrs. Pruitt said, "Travis announced to the garrison that they were on their own. Help would not be coming, not in the time needed. Then he listed their options. Surrendering would be pointless, he told them. Santa Anna would have them killed for sure if they did. Slipping through the Mexican lines was almost impossible."

Raquel sat at her desk, eyeing her teacher with resentment. A spasm of anger and pent-up frustration crossed her face. She'd heard this whole story before. She hadn't liked it then, and she didn't like it now.

"Travis made it clear to everyone that they were doomed." Mrs. Pruitt's voice cracked. Her eyes became watery.

Marco listened intently, mesmerized by her lesson. He could only imagine what it must have been like for those Texans—Crockett, Travis, Dickenson, Bowie, and all the others to know that they were going to die, to know that none of them had a chance of survival. What a tremendous amount of courage it must have taken for them to remain at the Alamo and fight.

Marco knew about courage. His grandfather preached it all the time. "You gotta look Fear in the face and let it know you ain't scared, Marco. Only then will you be ready to win."

Looking Fear in the face was one thing. Staring down Death took courage to a whole different level.

"Travis unsheathed his sword and drew a long line in the dirt," Mrs. Pruitt said. She pantomimed drawing a line on the floor in front of her students. "He told his men that he was prepared to fight to the death. Then he invited anyone who wanted to join him to step over." She stuck her chin up in the air and smiled. "And without hesitation, one by one, each man crossed the line. Even Bowie, who was too weak to walk, said, 'I don't know how much good I'll do you, but here's another life for Texas.' He had some men carry him across."

Marco imagined how that scene would be played out in the Alamo program. He'd lay on a cot, weakened, but still willing to fight. He'd wave his Bowie knife in the air as he was carried over. He assumed he would be provided with a Bowie knife—a prop rubber one of course. He couldn't wait for the night of the performance.

"Finally, after twelve days of intense fighting, the Mexican Army charged the Alamo for the last time." Mrs. Pruitt paced in front of the class like a revival tent preacher. Her hands were balled up into fists. Her voice grew louder. "With the last ounce of their strength, almost two hundred Texas heroes valiantly fought Santa Anna's forces, giving their lives for the right to be free. To be free from Mexico's oppression."

"Mrs. Pruitt?"

The teacher paused. She glimpsed at Raquel Flores from above the rim of her glasses. "Did you say something?" She was surprised to hear her voice. Raquel hardly ever said anything in class.

"She's a good girl. Real quiet," Mrs. Pruitt had told Raquel's parents through an interpreter on Parent Conference Night.

Raquel sat up. "Why don't you tell the class the real truth about the Alamo?"

Mrs. Pruitt looked at her, baffled. "I'm sorry?"

"Tell the class about the U.S. immigrants who crossed over to Mexico looking for a better life. But once they settled there, they didn't learn the language. They didn't adapt to the culture. And they didn't obey the laws of the country."

Raquel's feelings that she'd long kept suppressed poured out. They had been bubbling inside her for days. But up until now, only her diary knew about them.

"Tell the class about how the Mexican government had to pass new laws to stop U.S. immigration. But they still continued to cross over . . . *illegally*! Then they started protesting, demanding their civil rights. Finally, they decided to take land that didn't belong to them to form their own country!"

Some of the kids applauded. Some kids booed.

Mrs. Pruitt drew back, clearly uncomfortable. No one had ever questioned her lessons.

Raquel heaved heavy, shaky breaths. She couldn't believe what she'd just done. She hadn't intended to lash out at her teacher. But she had found the whole lesson infuriating. Maybe it was hearing Izzy and Orlando and Felipe reciting that insulting cartoon dialogue in the Alamo program. That certainly added to her anger. Maybe it was all the recent talk on the news about immigration issues. She was sick of her family living in constant fear, always worrying about being arrested and being deported.

"You call Crockett, Travis, and Bowie heroes," Raquel continued. "But the Mexican soldiers were even bigger heroes, Mrs. Pruitt. They died defending my country against U.S. rebels."

"Now hold on just a minute, young lady!" Mrs. Pruitt snapped. Ordinarily, she didn't have a problem with students expressing their opinions. She usually welcomed them. They made for good classroom discussions. But Raquel was pushing the wrong buttons. "Perhaps you need to go back and reread chapter nine. Because you seem to have forgotten that there were a number of Mexicans — Tejanos — who fought at the Alamo. And Lorenzo de Zavala, another Mexican, was one of the signers of the Texas Declaration of Independence. Not only that, he also served as interim vice president of the Republic of Texas. What do you call those men?"

"I call them sellouts!" Raquel answered without hesitation.

The kids snickered.

But Raquel hadn't said it to be funny. "You say Texans fought for freedom. Of course they did. For the freedom to keep their slaves. For the freedom to disobey Mexican laws. For the freedom to steal land that didn't belong to them. For the freedom to . . ."

"That's enough, Raquel!" Mrs. Pruitt's face burned with indignation. "Maybe that's the way they teach this in Mexico, but that's not the way we teach it here in the USA!"

Then she rattled off something else, but Raquel missed it. She turned her head away in angry defiance.

After class, Marco caught up with her. "Man, what did you eat for breakfast?"

Raquel glared at him. "Why didn't *you* speak up, Marco? Why didn't you defend me? You're supposed to be my friend."

He froze.

"You sat there like a *tonto* and said nothing!"

Her words stung him like angry wasps. "Well, wh . . . what was I supposed to say?" he sputtered. "That I agree with you? That I think the Texans were the bad guys and the Mexicans were the good guys?"

"But it's the truth, Marco. You know it is!"

"No, Raquel, that's your truth. Not mine!"

Her eyes narrowed with contempt. "You can't possibly understand how I feel, Marco. But then, why should you? You were born here!"

The wasps stung him again. "Hey, don't take it out on me. I didn't do anything." He put his arm around her. "Come on, we're friends. Let's not fight. I gave you the teddy bear, didn't I?"

"This?" She stared at the black bear in her hand and snorted. "Take it. I don't want it." She jerked away from him and shoved the bear against his chest.

"Raquel . . . "

"Leave me alone!"

She stomped away and disappeared into a crowd of kids.

Marco lingered for a second. Then he trudged down the hallway to his next class with a wounded look in his eyes. The bear dangled at his side. *Man, I didn't know she was like that. Was I wrong about her!* He gazed down at the teddy bear. *And to think that I spent almost ten dollars on this. What an ingrate.*

CHAPTER EIGHTEEN

"Let's go over Scene Seven." Mrs. Frymire scanned the notes on her clipboard. "The Mexican Army has just attacked, and the Texans are trying to regroup."

Billy Ray Cansler as William B. Travis, Andy LaFleur as Almeron Dickenson, and Agatha Hornbuckle as Susanna Dickenson took the stage.

Billy Ray: "Cease fire! Cease fire! They're retreating! Looks like they've had enough for one day. Captain, have your men check the casualties. Get Doc Sanders to help you."

Andy: "Colonel! Look! Over at that church. They're raising a red flag."

Billy Ray: "I see it. The Mexicans are letting us know with that flag that they're not showing us any mercy, any quarter."

Andy: "We've gotta get the women and children outta here. Soldier! Gather 'em all and load 'em into wagons. Let's move 'em out as soon as possible."

Agatha: "Oh, Almeron, I'm not leaving you. I want to stay."

Andy: "Susanna, that's crazy. You saw what just happened. And that was nothing. The Mexicans will attack again at any moment, and it'll be much worse next time. I want you and Angelina out of here immediately."

Agatha: "Oh, Almeron, I'm not leaving you. I want to stay."

"Agatha?"

She looked down from the stage at Mrs. Frymire. "Yes?"

"You already said that line. Say the next part."

Agatha tried to remember what came next, but nothing came to mind. Her body stiffened, and she balled her hands into tight fists. "Um, Mrs. Frymire, could you please help me with the first few words?"

"I'm so worried."

Agatha's face grew pale. "Please don't be worried, Mrs. Frymire. I'll learn all my lines. I promise."

"No, Agatha. 'I'm so worried' is your next line."

"It is?"

"I'm so worried. The Mexicans scare me," Mrs. Frymire read from the script.

Agatha stared blankly.

"Say it, Agatha. Say, 'I'm so worried. The Mexicans scare me.'"

"I'm so worried. The Mexicans scare me."

"That red flag scares me."

"That red flag scares me," Agatha echoed.

"But I know you're just as frightened as I am."

"But I know . . . "

" . . . you're just as frightened as I am."

"You're just as frightened as I am."

Marco couldn't believe Agatha had been given the part of Susanna Dickenson. She couldn't act at all. Raquel would've done a ten times better job than her. But then, he thought, Blanca's cabbit could've done a better job.

He looked around the auditorium for Raquel, but she wasn't there. He didn't understand why she'd gotten all steamed up during Texas history class. Why did she have to challenge Mrs. Pruitt? Then get mad at him for not siding with her? Raquel wasn't even in the United States legally.

She'd never told him that, but he knew. At home, Marco's dad sometimes talked about the guys at work. A couple of them, he said, were illegal immigrants. One of them was a man named Gustavo Sánchez. Everybody called him Flaco. The other one was Emilio Flores, Raquel's father.

Not that it mattered to Marco. He didn't care if Raquel was here legally or not. It was none of his business. But sometimes she got on his nerves, especially when she brought up touchy subjects—like immigration. Raquel had blathered on and on about the protest march in Dallas. Marco pretended to be interested, but the rally hadn't really meant anything to him.

"You can't possibly understand how I feel, Marco. But then, why should you? You were born here!"

Maybe there was some truth to that, he thought.

"Okay, that's fine for now," Mrs. Frymire told the group. "Keep working on your part, Agatha. Now let's go back to Scene Three. This is where the Mexicans first arrive." She called Billy Ray, Moe, and Marco to the stage.

Billy Ray: "Well, they finally made it. Take a good look, men. That's our opposition out there."

Moe, as Davy Crockett, aimed his imaginary rifle. "Which one's Santy Anny? Ol' Betsy here's just itching to get to know 'im better."

Marco as Jim Bowie: "Colonel! A group of 'em's heading this way! Get ready!"

Billy Ray: "Wait! Don't shoot! They're waving a white flag of truce. Let's see what they want."

Izzy and Orlando walked upstage and stopped in front of the Texans.

Orlando: General Antonio López de Santa Anna, de President of Mexico, sends dees messich to de commander off de Alamo."

Izzy: "Jew are hereby ordered to leef dees meeshun at once. Eef dees order ees not obeyed, we weel deestroy de Alamo and all off de occupants een eet."

Billy Ray hee-hawed. "The only thing you guys are gonna destroy is the English language."

Izzy sneered at him. "Maybe so, but you'll still be a buck-toothed, bald-headed orangutan!"

Everybody laughed.

Izzy crouched down, scratched his sides, and made monkey sounds.

"You're a real funny guy, aren't you?" Billy Ray said. "Let's see how funny you'll be without any teeth!"

Marco quickly stepped between them. "I told you to leave Izzy alone."

"Shut up, Marco, unless you want some of this, too." Billy Ray pounded his fist on his palm.

Mrs. Frymire threw her hands up in the air. "Stop it! All of you. I am not going to tolerate any threats."

"Then tell him to stop calling me that!" Billy Ray cried.

"You mean a buck-toothed, bald-headed orangutan?" Izzy laughed hysterically.

Marco yanked him by the arm and whispered, "Cut it out, man!"

"Okay, that's it!" Mrs. Frymire said. "Rehearsal's over. I'll see all of you again tomorrow afternoon."

"I'll escort the boys out of the building," Mr. Watts offered. "Billy Ray, you wait here. Marco, you, Izzy, Orlando, and Felipe come with me."

As they walked out of the auditorium, Izzy turned around and wiggled his fingers at Billy Ray. "Bye-bye, you buck-toothed, bald-headed orangutan!"

CHAPTER NINETEEN

"Knock, knock." An attractive, slender woman with short blond hair stood at Ms. Martínez's door. Chiseled face with high cheekbones, an upturned nose, and a delicate chin, she resembled a life-sized Barbie doll. She wore a lilac-colored blazer with a white blouse underneath and a lime-green skirt. The skirt, which was high above her knees, would have found her in violation of the school dress code if she were a Rosemont student. The woman held a white wicker basket in her hand. Lilac and lime-green tissue paper partially hid lilac and lime-green plastic bottles inside the basket.

"Hi, I'm Darlene Hornbuckle, Agatha's mother."

Ms. Martínez rose from her desk. "A pleasure to meet you, Mrs. Hornbuckle. Thank you for coming."

Mrs. Hornbuckle handed her the wicker basket. "I brought you a small gift I thought you might enjoy. It's from the Trudy Carlisle Collection. You know, Trudy Carlisle? Skin Care with Style? I'm a Trudy Carlisle beauty consultant." She pointed to a gold pin on the lapel of her blazer. The pin had a T and a C separated by a picture of a tube of lipstick.

Ms. Martínez peered inside the basket.

"There's a body wash, a moisture lotion, and a fragrant spray," Mrs. Hornbuckle pointed out. "Do you use Trudy Carlisle?"

Ms. Martínez smiled. "No, but I will now."

"A number of teachers here at Rosemont, including Mrs. Frymire and Mrs. Pruitt, are clients of mine," Mrs. Hornbuckle said. "Miss Mac, too, before . . . " Her eyes took on an appropriate, sorrowful look. Then she composed herself. "Here's my card. And a brochure. Let me know if I can assist you with any of our products."

Ms. Martínez placed the card, the brochure, and the gift basket on her desk. She scooped up the test papers she had been grading and placed them, face down, on the far end. Then she invited Agatha's mother to sit down.

"Ms. Martínez, I want you to know that Agatha is very excited about having you as her teacher. As I'm sure you can imagine, we were devastated by Miss Mac's untimely death. She was a great person. Then we worried about who was going to replace her. But after Agatha's first day in your class, she came home raving about you." Mrs. Hornbuckle flashed a big, wide, Trudy Carlisle beauty consultant smile. "About how pretty you looked and what a sweet disposition you have." Her smile turned sheepish. "I hope you won't take this the wrong way, Ms. Martínez, but Agatha had been a little concerned at first because . . . well, she's never had a Spanish teacher before and . . . "

"I'm not a Spanish teacher, Mrs. Hornbuckle," Ms. Martínez corrected her in a half-serious, half-kidding tone. "I'm an English teacher. Mr. Segovia is the Spanish teacher at our school. But I don't think Agatha is taking Spanish this year."

Mrs. Hornbuckle's eyes became blank, as if someone had suddenly flashed a bright light in her face. "Uh, well, no. What I mean to say is . . . " A nervous giggle escaped from her mouth. "Anyway, Agatha's had nothing but nice things to say about you."

Ms. Martínez folded her hands on her desk. Then in a sober tone she said, "You received the potential failing notice, didn't you?"

Mrs. Hornbuckle crossed her legs and adjusted her skirt. "Ms. Martínez, Agatha's never been much of a reader. I mean, it's not as if she doesn't know how to read. But with cheerleading practice and her babysitting jobs, she doesn't have a lot of time to sit down with a book. Plus, she also helps me with my beauty shows."

Ms. Martínez said, "I understand how busy Agatha is, Mrs. Hornbuckle. Unfortunately, her problem is more than just cracking open a book. Agatha has four missing reading assignments. She had a 75 to begin with, but now, with four zeroes, she's in grave danger of failing."

Mrs. Hornbuckle uncrossed her legs, then crossed them again. She tugged at her skirt and placed her hands on her lap. "You say she had a 75?" Another Trudy Carlisle smile spread across her face. "Well, there you go. That shows you Agatha can do the work. And after all, isn't that what you're trying to find out? To see if Agatha can read? Why don't we just leave her grade at a 75? What do you say?" She gave the teacher a conspiratorial wink.

Ms. Martínez shook her head. "I'm afraid it doesn't quite work that way, Mrs. Hornbuckle."

"Then what about her part in the Alamo play? Agatha's done a lot of reading for that. Mrs. Frymire has told me that Agatha's been working very hard to learn her lines. I'm sure you can give her extra credit for it."

"The play has nothing to do with my English class," Ms. Martínez said with a sigh.

Mrs. Hornbuckle frowned. "It did when Miss Mac was the teacher. She used to give extra credit to any student who participated in one of her plays. I should know.

I was in one of them. Did Agatha tell you that Miss Mac was my teacher when I was a little girl?"

Ms. Martínez gazed impatiently around the room. "No, she didn't."

"When I was in her class, Miss Mac wrote and directed a beautiful Christmas pageant. I played the part of the angel who announced to the shepherds the birth of baby Jesus." She turned her eyes to the ceiling. Then she lifted her hands in the air like a football referee signaling a touchdown. "Fear not, for behold, I bring you good tidings of great joy, which shall be to all people. For unto you is born this day in the city of David a Savior, which is Christ the Lord." She paused and waited for Ms. Martínez's reaction, but the teacher remained silent. "Of course, you can't do plays like that anymore, not with everybody trying to be politically correct." She made quotation marks in the air with her fingers. "And last year, my daughter Brenda played Titania in Miss Mac's marvelous presentation of Shakespeare's *A Midsummer Night's Dream*. She had to memorize pages and pages of dialogue for her role. She did it in such a short time, too."

"Mrs. Hornbuckle, if Agatha wants to pass this grading period," Ms. Martínez said bluntly, "she will have to stay after school with me every afternoon to make up her work. Otherwise the four zeroes will be averaged in as part of her final grade."

Mrs. Hornbuckle's lips tried for another Trudy Carlisle smile, but this time they malfunctioned. "But if she does that, Agatha won't be able to attend the rehearsals for the play."

Ms. Martínez shrugged with indifference. "Then perhaps she shouldn't be in it. Right now I'm more concerned about her grade than her part in the show."

She rose from her chair. "You'll have to excuse me, Mrs. Hornbuckle, but I need to get ready for my next class. My students will be arriving at any moment."

Agatha's mother stood up, her face flushed with indignation. "Don't you think you're being unfair to everyone involved in the play? I mean, if Agatha's not in it, who's going to replace her?"

Ms. Martínez motioned toward the door with an open hand. "Thank you for coming by, Mrs. Hornbuckle."

The friendly façade on Agatha's mother's face was now replaced with a cold, venomous stare. "You're not pulling Agatha out of the program, you hear?" she bellowed. "She's going to be in it whether you like it or not. I'm going to have a talk with Mrs. Frymire about this!"

She snatched the Trudy Carlisle gift basket from the desk and bolted out of the room.

Ms. Martínez stood at the door with her arms crossed and watched her storm down the hallway. *I wonder how many Trudy Carlisle products it cost you to buy Agatha the part in the play, Mrs. Hornbuckle.*

CHAPTER TWENTY

People in Texas are fond of saying, "If you don't like the weather here, wait five minutes and it'll change."

It took a little longer than five minutes, but not much more.

Sunday, the high had been a balmy 69 degrees, unseasonably warm weather for February.

On Monday morning, however, a blast of Arctic winds slammed into the area, packing a wintry mix of snow, sleet, and ice. It dropped temperatures to a frigid 18 degrees, with wind chills dipping into the single digits.

Izzy Peña was out of bed early. He wrapped himself in his blanket and sat on the couch in the living room with his feet tucked under his legs. He turned on the TV to Channel Eight "The News That Can't Wait." He crossed his fingers and waited anxiously for reports of school closings.

The night before, Dana Shackelford, the Channel Eight weather forecaster, had predicted the drastic changes in temperature. She said to expect icy drizzle and freezing rain mixed with snow by morning.

Izzy knew icy drizzle and freezing rain meant icy road conditions. And icy road conditions probably meant school buses would not be running. And no school buses running surely meant no school.

On television, Izzy watched a news reporter named Melinda Trice, dressed in a heavy, black, wool coat standing alongside a highway. She pointed to sanding trucks and explained that maintenance crews had been working all morning to cover the slippery roads with a mixture of salt and sand, giving special attention to bridges and overpasses.

The news switched to another reporter, a middle-aged man with salt-and-pepper hair named Ron Cowart. He was at the scene of a five-car pileup, describing how treacherous the driving conditions were. One of the vehicles, a green SUV, was flipped upside down with its air bags deployed. Ron Cowart urged motorists not to leave the house unless they absolutely had to.

Izzy thought the car accidents looked cool. But that wasn't why he was watching the news. All he cared about at the moment was whether or not he would have to go to school.

The studio switched back to Melinda Trice, who repeated what she'd already stated about the sanding trucks.

It then showed another reporter flying in a helicopter. The reporter offered a bird's-eye view of traffic conditions around the city. The sun had not risen, and the cars looked like twinkling stars against a black, patent leather highway.

The weather forecaster appeared next. Dana Shackelford gave an update on weather conditions, using words that made no sense to Izzy. Words like barometer, dew point, and Doppler radar. She pointed to a gigantic map of the United States. It was decorated with pictures of snowflakes, clouds, and giant H and L letters. The weather forecaster swept her hand across the map in a circular motion and used more words Izzy didn't understand. High pressure system. Air mass. Humidity.

"Who cares?" Izzy said aloud. "Is there going to be school today? That's all I want to know!"

Finally, fifteen minutes after he turned on the television, Izzy was rewarded with the news he'd been waiting to hear.

"Yes!" He bounced off the couch. "Mami! Blanca! Come here. Hurry! There's no school today!"

Ms. Peña rushed into the living room. She held her robe tightly around her waist as she reached for the ends of her belt to tie it together. Her dark-brown hair stood straight up as if she'd stuck her finger into an electric socket.

"*¿Qué pasó, muchacho? ¿Por qué estás gritando?*"

Izzy pointed at the TV screen. "Mami, they just announced on the news that there's no school today!"

Ms. Peña groaned. "*Ay, m'ijo.* I knew that. I heard it on the radio about thirty minutes ago."

"You did? Then why didn't you tell me?"

"Because I wanted to let you and Blanca sleep a little longer." She walked barefoot across the cold linoleum floor to the window and drew open the curtains. A white sheet of snow blanketed the tiny front yard. The limbs on the trees, having been stripped of their leaves since early December, were coated with translucent layers of ice. A mild breeze pelted the window with tiny specks of sleet.

The sun was beginning to rise, revealing a dirty gray sky that would fade to a lighter tint as the day progressed.

Staring at the icy street in front of her house, she considered calling her boss to say she wouldn't be able to make it to work. It might even be true. She didn't know if her car, a 1997 Ford Taurus, would start.

Izzy's mother worked as a waitress at a Mexican restaurant called La Paloma Blanca. She clocked in at ten in the morning and worked until two o'clock. After that, she went home for a short break. She returned to the restaurant at five o'clock and worked until the restaurant closed at ten.

Izzy and Blanca sometimes waited up for her. She'd come home at the end of the day, exhausted and smelling of Mexican food and tortilla chips. The three of them would gather at the kitchen table. Izzy and Blanca marveled as their mother dug into the pockets of her waitress uniform, a red pleated skirt with a white blouse, and brought out wads of dollar bills and coins, the evening's worth of tips. Piled on top of the table, the money looked like a small fortune. But the harsh reality was that it barely paid the bills.

On her days off, she worked at home as a seamstress, repairing torn clothing and making alterations. Occasionally, she sewed dresses for proms and *quinceañeras*. Most of her work came from friends and friends of friends.

If she stayed home, she could work on the costumes for Izzy's Alamo program. She had already sewn about half of them.

Ms. Peña changed her mind about calling in sick. Her boss, Mingo Salazar, would be counting on her to show up. On days like this, business was impossible to predict. Either it would be dead, with most people heeding the weather forecaster's warning to stay home, or the restaurant would be packed with customers hungering for hot Mexican food.

Izzy joined his mother at the window. This was the first real snow they'd seen this winter. Back in December, a few snow flurries had fallen. There was even talk on the news of a possible white Christmas. Unfortunately, by Christmas morning, the snow had melted completely.

But today there was enough snow to build a snowman. A good-sized one, too.

"Go back to sleep, *m'ijo*," Ms. Peña said. "Maybe later, you and Blanca can go outside and play."

Izzy glanced at the clock. It was almost seven o'clock. There was no need to be up, now that he had learned what he needed to know. He retreated to his room and stayed in bed for the next three hours.

CHAPTER TWENTY-ONE

It was the dead silence in the house that stirred Izzy from his sleep. He sat up in his bed and listened for sounds of movement outside his door.

Nothing.

It took a moment for him to remember that there was no school. He looked at his window. It was covered with frost, blocking his view to the outside. He got out of bed and walked to the living room. He expected Blanca to be sitting on the couch watching television. The room was empty.

He checked the kitchen. Nobody was there either.

He stopped outside his mother's bedroom door. "Mami?" No response.

He rapped twice, then opened it. She was gone.

He opened Blanca's door, which was next to his mother's. The room was straightened up and the bed was made, as if it had not been slept in. A white teddy bear that Blanca had won at the state fair sat on top of the bed.

The bathroom door down the hall was closed. Izzy knocked. "Hey, Blanc, you in there?"

He opened it, expecting to find his sister sitting on the toilet. Nothing.

He flipped on the light, just to make sure. The bathroom was just as empty with the light on as it was with the light off. A weird, unsettling feeling washed over Izzy. He felt as if he was the last person on earth.

He recalled a warning he'd heard from a TV preacher his mom liked to watch, Brother Clyde Vincent. Brother Clyde talked about something called the Rupture. Or was it the Rapture? According to Brother Clyde, in the end of days, during the Rupture or the Rapture, the hand of God would reach down and carry all the good people up to Heaven. All the bad ones would remain on earth. Izzy couldn't remember what the preacher said would happen to those left behind, but he knew it couldn't be good. After all, if God didn't want them in Heaven with him, what was the alternative?

Izzy and his family never went to church. His mother worked on Sundays. But she always watched Brother Clyde on TV. She even sent him money when the tips were good. The hand of God, Izzy knew, would surely take his mom during the Rupture/Rapture.

He hated to admit it but Blanca would probably go, too. She never did anything wrong. He couldn't even think of any sins she was capable of committing. She was too young to do anything really bad.

As for him . . . Izzy suddenly wished he had been nicer to his sister. He wished he had offered to help her catch the cabbit, even if it turned out to be nothing more than a long-eared cat. He wished he hadn't . . .

The front door flew open. Blanca rushed inside and headed toward the kitchen.

"Morning, Izzy."

He snapped out of his trance-like state. "Where were you?"

"Outside making a snowman." Blanca opened the refrigerator and grabbed a carrot from the vegetable bin. "This is for his nose. Wanna help?"

Without giving it a second thought, Izzy said, "Sure. Where's Mami?"

"She left for work about a half hour ago."

Izzy looked up at the clock. He didn't realize he had slept that long. "I'll be out there in a few minutes."

He got dressed. He zipped up his thick brown jacket and added a scarf around his neck. He slipped on his gloves and covered his head with a navy-blue wool cap.

When he got outside, Blanca was adding tree branches for arms to her snowman.

He stared at the blob of snow that barely resembled a snowman. It looked more like a snowy version of Jabba the Hut, the creature from Star Wars.

But he didn't tell her that. He didn't want to say anything negative. Just in case.

"Here. Let's put this on him." Izzy removed his scarf and wrapped it around the snowman's neck, or what he thought was the snowman's neck. It was hard to tell.

"Get the broom from the pantry. We'll lean it against his arm. Then he'll be complete."

While Blanca ran inside to get the broom, Izzy smoothed the edges, rounding each section, trying to give it a more defined semblance of a snowman.

Whack!

A snowball, which was mostly composed of ice, struck him on the back of his head with such force that it made him stagger. Izzy had to grab onto the snowman to keep from falling. He turned around as another snowball zipped toward him and smacked him on the chest.

Billy Ray Cansler, Luther Bowers, and Joshua and Jacob Bukowski were standing on the sidewalk in front of Izzy's house.

"Would you like me to help you with your snowman, little boy?" Billy Ray asked in a mocking voice. His gang laughed.

"Leave me alone, Billy Ray!" Izzy stepped back, prepared to run if he had to.

"Hey, no problem, amigo. I just stopped by to help you with your snowman." He grabbed the snowman's head and yanked it off.

"There. It looks much better," he said, throwing the head on the ground.

The glob of snow, with its two black button eyes and carrot nose, gazed up without expression.

"Hey, that's my sister's snowman!"

"It *was* your sister's snowman." Billy Ray threw his shoulder against the remainder of the snowman and leveled it with a body block, leaving only a small white hill.

"Call me a buck-toothed, bald-headed orangutan again, you pinhead. Come on, say it to my face." He gave Izzy a hard shove. "You're not so tough now without your girlfriend Marco Díaz at your side, are you?"

Before Izzy could answer, Luther Bowers hit him on the ear with a snowball.

Whack!

Whack! Whack!

The Bukowskis hit their target, one on the face and the other on Izzy's chest.

In a panic, Izzy tore out of the yard.

Down the sidewalk he ran, with Billy Ray and his gang hurling snowballs at him. One caught him on the shoulder; another one hit him on the back of his neck.

"Yeah, you'd better run!" Billy Ray yelled.

Izzy sped toward the construction site. Maybe Marco would be there. He rounded the corner and saw a group of kids. They were sliding down a hill on a makeshift cardboard sled. Unfortunately Marco wasn't with them. Izzy stopped at the building frame and turned around.

Whack!

A snowball tagged him hard on the face.

He glanced past the steel structure and discovered he was trapped. The wooden fence, too high for him to climb, blocked any possible exit. The cabbit may have been able to scramble underneath it, but Izzy would never fit.

He had an idea. If he scaled up the building frame and Billy Ray and his gang climbed up after him, he could leap off onto the sand pile and get away. He'd do it with ease. He'd done it a million times. He knew Billy Ray and his gang wouldn't jump off as effortlessly. It was a long way down. They'd probably be scared to even try. It had taken Izzy and Marco a while to build up enough courage to attempt it the first time.

Their reluctance to jump would be all the time Izzy would need to get away. Then he'd run back home. Or maybe he'd head over to Marco's.

He shinnied up a girder. He could feel the coldness of the steel even through his gloves. He made it to the second floor.

Billy Ray and his gang stopped at the foot of the building. "Now we've got you!"

Come on, climb up here, you buck-toothed, bald-headed orangutan! Climb on up and we'll see who's got who.

To Izzy's horror, Billy Ray and his gang didn't try to climb up the building.

"Thanks for making yourself such an easy target, idiot!" Billy Ray gathered up a handful of snow and shaped it into a ball. Then he fired.

Izzy clung to the girder as he dodged the snowball. Luther and the Bukowskis tossed another volley of snowballs. Izzy swung around, trying his best to avoid getting hit.

He peered down at the sand pile. He could still leap off and make his getaway. Billy Ray and his gang wouldn't expect him to jump. Not from this high up.

He released the girder. Carefully he crossed the beam, ballencing himself like a tightrope walker. Another few feet and he'd be directly above the sand pile.

Whack!

The snowball hit Izzy flush in the eyes. Instinctively, he reached for his face. As he did, he lost his ballence, slipping on the slick, steel surface.

He fell, banging his head against a beam on the way down. He landed limply on the ground with a painful thud.

Izzy lay dazed and disoriented. His head throbbed with a sharp, stinging pulse. Blood poured freely from a cut just above his right eye. It streamed down to the white ground, coating it like a snow cone with a brilliant shade of red.

The world became blurry. Izzy could feel the ground spinning. He gazed up at the large gray clouds hanging above him.

The last thing he saw before he passed out was the hand of God reaching down for him.

CHAPTER TWENTY-TWO

"He's suffered a concussion," the doctor told Izzy's mother. "The worst of it is the gash, but we'll take care of it easy enough. All in all, I'd say your boy was pretty lucky."

Lucky? Stretched out on a hospital bed with his forehead about to be stitched up, Izzy didn't feel lucky at all.

"Will he have to spend the night here?" Ms. Peña asked, "'cause I ain't got no insurance and . . ."

"No. After we suture the wound, he'll be ready to go home."

It was Blanca who had found him. From the living room window, she had seen Billy Ray and his gang harassing her brother. When they started chasing him, she followed them to the construction site.

After Izzy fell, Billy Ray and his gang ran away. Blanca rushed over to him. He was unconscious and bleeding profusely from a deep cut on his forehead. She tried to revive him by smearing snow on his face.

Finally, he began to stir.

She helped him to his feet and walked him home, with Izzy leaving a thin trail of blood behind them. She called her mom at work and explained what happened. When their mother arrived, Blanca was dropped off at her friend Teresa's house, and Izzy was driven to the hospital.

The doctor stroked Izzy's hair while the nurse cleaned the wound. "I'm going to give you an injection, an anesthetic," he said. "Now I won't lie to you, son. It's going to sting. But after that, you won't feel a thing, okay?"

Izzy nodded weakly. He undid his cuff button and started to roll up his sleeve.

"Oh, I'm sorry. I didn't make myself clear," the doctor said. "I'm not giving you a shot on the arm."

Not on his arm? Then where? On his butt? No way. It'll be so embarrassing! This'll be worse than falling off the building.

"You'd better steady his head, Fran," the doctor told the nurse.

The nurse, wearing latex gloves, grabbed the sides of Izzy's head while the doctor prepared the syringe and needle.

"What are you going to do?" Izzy wailed with a growing fear.

"Hold him still." The doctor plunged the needle into the cut.

"Aaahh! No! It hurts! It hurts!" Izzy flailed his legs. He tried to jerk his head, but the nurse's grip was too strong.

His mother, still in her waitress uniform, turned her face and cowered in the corner as she listened to her son's screams.

There was another injection. Then one more.

"That's it," the doctor said at last. "Now that wasn't so bad, was it?"

After a couple of minutes, the pain was gone. The doctor then meticulously sutured the wound. Izzy couldn't believe what was happening to him. He was getting sewn up! He could see the doctor working over him, but he hardly felt a thing. There was only a slight pressure when the needle, which looked more like a type of fishing hook, tugged at his skin.

When the doctor was finished, the nurse released her grip. She cleaned Izzy's head, then applied a bandage over the cut.

"How many stitches did it take to close it up, doctor?" Ms. Peña asked. Her stomach was still queasy.

"Fifteen, I think. Yes, eight on the inside and the rest on the outside. It was a pretty nasty wound." He removed his gloves and dropped them into a medical wastebasket.

Ms. Peña tottered unsteadily toward her son. "*Ay, m'ijo.*"

"You'll need to keep him off his feet for a day or so," the doctor advised. "Give his wound a chance to heal. Also, keep an eye out for signs of dizziness, nausea, or confusion. I'll give you a prescription for antibiotics to keep the wound from getting infected. I'll give you another one for the pain." The doctor rose and headed for the door. "I want to see him in a week to make sure the wound is healing properly. Fran will take care of you from here on." Then he left.

"Mami, I'm sorry," Izzy apologized. "I know I shouldn't have been at the construction site." He started to cry.

"Let's not talk about it right now," his mother said. "The important thing is that you're okay. We can talk later. Right now, let's just get you home."

Twenty minutes later, Blanca saw the car pull into the driveway. She flew out of Teresa's house and ran to meet them. She opened the passenger door and saw her brother slumped over.

Terrified, she whispered, "Mami, is Izzy all right?"

"Yeah, I'm fine," Izzy answered. He sat up. "Here, help me out."

"Let me do that." His mother came around to his side. Teresa's mother approached the car as Izzy climbed out. "How's Izzy?"

Ms. Peña offered a faint smile. "He's a little banged up, but he'll be fine."

"Your brother looks like he was in a war," Teresa told Blanca.

"I know. Come on, I want to see him in the light." The girls followed Izzy inside the house.

"Teresa! Come back here," her mother called. "Izzy needs to rest."

A few seconds later, Teresa poked her head out the door. "Come take a look at Izzy, Ma. This is so neat. He looks like somebody beat him up or something."

"Teresa!"

"But he does!"

"Let's go. Now!"

Ms. Peña hugged Teresa's mother. "Carol, I really appreciate you watching after Blanca while we were at the hospital."

"Oh, sure, no problem. Call me if you need anything, okay? Teresa!"

"I'm coming!"

Izzy lay on the sofa in the living room. His mother sat on the love seat next to him. It was almost time for her evening shift. The restaurant had been swamped with customers during lunch, despite the ice and snow. Her boss anticipated it to be just as packed at night. She hated to leave Mingo Salazar shorthanded, but right now her priority was her son. She asked Blanca to fill a glass with water so Izzy could take the sample pain tablets the nurse had given him.

Blanca handed her brother the glass. "Why were Billy Ray and his friends chasing you?"

Izzy washed two tablets down his throat with a drink of water. He leaned his head back against the arm of the sofa and closed his eyes. "It's a long story."

His mother took the glass and sat it on the coffee table. She unfolded a Mexican flag pattern quilt she kept on the sofa and covered him up with it. "I want you to give me the names of the boys who did this to you," she demanded. "They're not gonna get away with it."

Izzy muttered something, but his voice was barely audible.

"It was Billy Ray Cansler and three other boys," Blanca answered for Izzy.

"Who are those other boys? I want all their names."

Blanca shrugged. "The only one I know is Billy Ray."

Ms. Peña looked down at her son, but Izzy didn't say anything. "I'm gonna call the school first thing in the morning and report them to the principal. They're not gonna get away with this. *¡Muchachos sin vergüenza!*"

CHAPTER TWENTY-THREE

Marco Díaz was looking for Billy Ray Cansler. His heart pulsated with anger. He wasn't sure what he would do or say once he found him. His first instinct was to beat him up. Bust his head open just like Billy Ray had done to Izzy. But deep inside, he knew he wouldn't do that. For one thing, Marco didn't want to risk getting suspended. For another, he tried not to fight outside the ring. Boxing was a sport, an art, as his grandfather often described it. But brawling in the school yard was stupid. Still, he couldn't let Billy Ray get away with what he'd done. Even if Izzy had brought the whole thing on himself. He'd tried to warn him. If only Izzy could learn to control his big mouth.

Marco spotted Billy Ray and Luther Bowers hiding behind a leafless oak tree near the auditorium.

Billy Ray scooped up a handful of snow. He slipped away from the tree and snuck up behind Karen Ingram, shoving snow down the back of her shirt.

"Stop it!" Karen jerked away and brushed out the snow.

Billy Ray laughed like a loon. "I'm just trying to help you be cool, Karen—like me."

Whack!

The snowball caught Billy Ray on the back of his head. He spun around. "Who the . . . ?"

Marco Díaz was posed ominously against a parked car in front of the school. "Why don't you try to help *me* be cool, Billy Ray?"

Luther hustled to Billy Ray's side. He crouched down and picked up some snow.

"You do that and I'll cram that snowball down your throat," Marco threatened.

Luther dropped it immediately.

"L . . . Listen, man," Billy Ray blurted, "what happened to Izzy was an accident. It was his fault for climbing up that building."

Marco tromped up to him, stopping inches from his face. "You want to tell me why he felt the need to climb up that building in the first place?"

Billy Ray nervously retreated back a few steps. "Y . . . You trying to scare me or what?"

"Why?" Marco answered with a wild look in his eyes. "Do you feel scared?"

Billy Ray looked around the school yard. The Bukowski brothers had already gone home. The only person he had to back him up was Luther Bowers. That would make it a two-to-one fight. Even so, he didn't like the odds.

"I . . . I didn't touch Izzy or nothing. He slipped and fell off the building. Didn't he, Luther?"

Luther nodded.

"He slipped, huh?" In a flash, Marco assumed a boxing stance. He cocked his left arm and faked a jab.

Billy Ray jumped back. As he did, he lost his ballence on the slippery ground and fell, landing on his backside in a puddle of slush. He tried to scramble to his feet, but he fell down again. He flopped around in the melting snow like a fish out of water. Finally, he turned over on all fours and picked himself up.

"I see what you mean now, Billy Ray," Marco said with a twisted smile. "Izzy slipped. Just like you."

Billy Ray swiped the back of his wet pants.

"Next time, get yourself a pair of Pampers," Marco mocked. "That way, when you pee on yourself, it won't show through." He turned and walked away.

Luther and Billy Ray watched him as he crossed the street and turned the corner at the stop sign.

"You should've punched him in the mouth," Luther said. "That's what I would've done."

Billy Ray's eyes narrowed. "When the time's right." He swiped at his pants some more. "I would've done it now, but then he'd probably tell everybody that the only reason I was able to beat him up was because the ground was too slippery and he lost his ballence, or something stupid like that, the chicken. But this ain't over. It ain't over by a long shot."

CHAPTER TWENTY-FOUR

A black, Ford F-150 pickup truck pulled into the Rosemont School parking lot, taking up two spaces. The door on the driver's side sported a large, white decal with the words CANSLER CUSTOM HOMEBUILDING & REMODELING in red letters. The front left side of the truck was bashed in with the fender and the hood pushed up. The dent gave the truck the appearance of a bulldog with a vicious snarl.

Billy Ray Cansler's father stepped out. He wore black denim jeans, a matching black denim jacket, and a black, Panama, straw cowboy hat.

He took a final drag of his cigarette before tossing it in the snow and stamping it out with his boot.

Mr. Rathburn watched him through the window blinds.

"He's here."

"I'll get Ms. Peña." Ms. Martínez walked out of the conference room and summoned Izzy's mother, who had been sitting on a bench in the hallway for about ten minutes.

A few moments later there was a knock on the conference room door. Mr. Rathburn greeted Mr. Cansler, then invited him to join the TEAM 3 teachers and Izzy's mother at the table.

Keeping his hat on, Mr. Cansler took a seat next to Mrs. Frymire.

Mr. Rathburn opened a manila folder and pulled out a handful of files that included statements made by some of the teachers.

"Apparently, there's been some trouble brewing for quite a while between Billy Ray and Israel," he said in a serious tone. "I don't know who started it, and to be quite frank with you, it doesn't matter to me who did."

"I can tell you who started it!" Ms. Peña cried. "Billy Ray and some other boys have been picking on my son and his friends for a long time. They threatened to hurt Izzy, and finally they did!"

Mr. Cansler's face hardened. "Is that what your boy told you, ma'am? Did he also tell you that he's been calling Billy Ray names? Purposely riling him, humiliating him in front of everybody? He and that other Mexican boy, the boxer, have been trying to get Billy Ray to fight 'em. Now I've always told my son, 'Don't go looking for a fight, but if you find yourself in one, then you got every right to defend yourself.'"

"But your son wasn't defending himself!" Ms. Peña sputtered. "He and his friends attacked Izzy. They almost *killed* him!"

Mr. Cansler waved off her accusation with a flicker of his hand. "Don't exaggerate, ma'am. It was a snowball fight. All kids have 'em. Your boy's the one who climbed up that building and slipped off. You ain't gonna lay that blame on Billy Ray."

"Your son knocked him off!"

"He slipped! He shouldn't have been up there in the first place!"

"Hold it! Time out." Mr. Rathburn formed a T with his hands. "Mr. Cansler, Ms. Peña, let's try to maintain some dignity here, shall we? I did not bring you two so you could have a shouting match." He paused to give them a chance to cool down. "Like I was saying, it doesn't matter to me who started it. The point is that it's got to stop."

He shuffled the papers in his hands. "Now, Mr. Cansler, this is not the first time I've had to talk with you regarding Billy Ray's behavior. You'll recall, last November, your son was suspended for fighting."

"He didn't start that fight! Them boys he sometimes hangs around with, they started it. Billy Ray just happened to be there. But when he got slugged, what was he supposed to do? Like I said before, he has every right . . . "

"Then in January," Mr. Rathburn interrupted, "he was given an in-house suspension for popping firecrackers in the bathroom."

"He was just fooling around with some leftover firecrackers from New Year's Day. Don't tell me you never popped firecrackers when you was a boy."

"Not in the school bathrooms, sir," Mr. Rathburn said under his breath. He glanced through the rest of the files. "Then there was the stink bomb in the cafeteria, the dead rat . . . "

He sat the papers down and clasped his hands together. He gazed at Izzy's mother with sympathetic eyes. "Ms. Peña, I sincerely regret what happened to your son. I truly do. But, since the incident happened away from school, there's not much I can do about it."

Ms. Peña blinked incredulously. "What? Izzy had to go to the hospital! He's had to miss school, and I've had to take time off from work to take care of him, and you sit there and tell me you can't do anything about it?"

"He slipped!" Mr. Cansler interjected. "The metal beam he climbed up on was icy and he slipped. Why is that so hard for you to understand, ma'am?"

"Your son's a bully!"

Mr. Cansler crossed his arms defiantly and turned his head. "Let's wrap this up, boss," he told Mr. Rathburn. "I got more important things to do today. Some moron, who probably got his driver's license at the school for the blind and can't drive for spit, plowed into my pickup yesterday. I gotta see about getting it fixed."

Ms. Martínez raised her hand. "Mr. Rathburn, it seems that at every rehearsal, Billy Ray taunts Izzy. As far as I can tell, the comments Izzy has made have only been said in self-defense. Perhaps we need to pull Billy Ray out of the Alamo program."

Mr. Rathburn nodded. "That seems appropriate. At least it's a step in the right direction. Everybody in agreement with that?"

Mrs. Frymire and Mrs. Pruitt promptly beamed telepathic messages to each other.

"Excuse me, Mr. Rathburn," Mrs. Frymire said. "I think there are other ways we can resolve this without having to resort to pulling anyone out of the program."

"That's right," Mrs. Pruitt joined in. "We'll make sure to keep a closer watch on the boys."

Ms. Martínez flinched. She hadn't really expected the women to support her, but she didn't think they would contradict her in front of the parents. Mr. Watts sat in his chair, mute. He stared uncomfortably at the tabletop.

Mr. Cansler aimed a finger at the principal's face. "Understand this, boss. I agreed to build the Alamo façade for free. Ordinarily, I charge plenty of money to do that sort of work. But I ain't building nothing if Billy Ray's kicked off the show. You get me?"

"Well, if that bully stays in the program, I'm not gonna let Izzy be in it," Ms. Peña fumed. "And you can forget about me making your costumes!"

Mr. Cansler sneered. "Well, that's your prerogative, ma'am."

Mr. Rathburn turned a cold eye on him. He did not care for that man at all. Ms. Peña was right. Billy Ray was a bully, and it wasn't hard to tell where he picked up his habits.

If he could, he would transfer Billy Ray to an alternative school—the sort of place specifically set up for handling troublemakers. But district policy did not authorize him to do so. Not for an incident that happened off campus.

He stuffed the files back into the folder. "I'm going to fill out a report of our meeting this morning," he told the parents. "Each of you will receive a copy." Then he gave Mr. Cansler a stern warning. "If I have any more trouble with Billy Ray this year, I assure you, sir, that I will take stronger measures—*much stronger measures*—in dealing with him." He stood and smiled diplomatically. He gave the parents a cursory "thank you" for taking the time to attend the meeting.

"That's it?" an infuriated Ms. Peña spewed. "Izzy gets hurt, I have to take him to the hospital, and this is all you're gonna do about it? That's not right!" Her eyes watered up.

"I'm sorry, Ms. Peña." Mr. Rathburn stretched out his hand, but she refused to shake it. She bolted out of the conference room crying, "That's not right! That's not right!"

After the parents left, the teachers continued their discussion in the hallway.

"I told you Billy Ray was too unpredictable," Ms. Martínez said.

"We are not taking him out of the show, Sandy!" Mrs. Pruitt said gruffly. "Anyway, you heard what happened. Billy Ray didn't really do anything wrong. It was a snowball fight that got out of control."

Ms. Martínez's eyes widened. "Izzy's suffered a concussion. He has fifteen stitches on his head. And you're telling me that Billy Ray didn't do anything wrong?"

She could feel her heart palpitating with increased speed. Why was it that no matter how hard she tried, she could not get along with her coworkers?

"I'm not defending Billy Ray," Mrs. Frymire said, trying to sound impartial. "We know him all too well. But you have to admit that Izzy was the one who instigated this. We heard him teasing Billy Ray, insulting him, calling him a bald-headed baboon in front of everyone."

"Actually, he called him a buck-toothed, bald-headed orangutan," Mr. Watts corrected her.

Ms. Martínez glared at him.

"Hey, I'm just trying to keep the facts straight."

Ms. Martínez made a final plea. "John Ahne can take Billy Ray's place. I'm sure he knows the part. If not, it shouldn't take him long to memorize it."

Mrs. Pruitt smiled sarcastically. "Then who'll build the Alamo for us, Sandy? You?"

Mrs. Frymire folded her arms. "Billy Ray's staying in the play, and that's final. We're putting on the show in less than three weeks, and we're not changing a thing." She fixed an angry stare on Ms. Martínez. "Which reminds me, Mrs. Hornbuckle told me that you're trying to kick Agatha out of the play. Is that true?"

Ms. Martínez scowled. "No! But Agatha's failing, and she needs to come to my class for after-school tutoring."

Mrs. Frymire regarded her critically. "That still doesn't give you the authority to kick students out of the play."

"I didn't . . . " Ms. Martínez threw her hands up in resignation. "Fine. Do whatever you want. But leave me out of it." She stalked away, her heels striking the tile floor like ball peen hammers. And find someone else to teach the dances!"

Mr. Watts ran after her. "Sandy, wait up."

As they watched them leave, Mrs. Pruitt sniffed haughtily. *"That girl thinks she's all that and a bag of chips."*

CHAPTER TWENTY-FIVE

Lunchtime was the usual scene of organized chaos. Two enormous lines of loud, talkative students, impatiently waiting to be fed, snaked along the cafeteria walls. The food servers, in assembly-like fashion, kept the lines moving, feverishly doling out globs of mashed potatoes, sliced carrots, and little brown meat patties.

Raquel Flores stood outside the cafeteria doors and watched Marco make his way into the serving area near the front of a line.

As soon as Marco paid and sat down, Raquel entered the cafeteria. She sneaked a glance at Marco's table. Felipe and Orlando were sitting with him.

Once or twice, he looked up at her, but their eyes didn't meet.

"Hi, Raquel," a voice called from behind.

"Oh. Hi, Myra."

"Boy, I thought Mrs. Ledbetter was never going to let me leave the band room. What's for lunch? I'm starving."

"I don't know." Raquel looked across the room. She saw Judy Welch sitting near a window. Raquel considered joining her but quickly changed her mind. Judy was sitting with Billy Ray Cansler and Luther Bowers. *Ugh.*

"Mrs. Ledbetter thinks I can be first-chair clarinet if I practice enough, but I'm not really sure I want to continue playing the clarinet" Myra said. "I'd like to switch to the trumpet, but my mom won't let me. She says she spent a lot of money for my clarinet and that I can't keep changing my mind. So I guess I'm stuck playing the clarinet for now. But maybe later, when I get to high school and the clarinet's paid for, I can switch to the trumpet. What do you think?"

Raquel didn't answer. It didn't matter. Myra had plenty to say for the both of them.

"The reason Mrs. Ledbetter kept me a little late today was because I've been using a number two reed, and she thinks I would get a better sound if I used a two-and-a-half reed. I didn't think it would make that much of a difference, but I went ahead and tried one. And guess what? It was a great improvement. I get a much better sound out of a two-and-a-half reed than I did with my two reed."

Would you shut up? Raquel wanted to say. She tried her best to ignore her, but Myra, whose voice she had once described to Marco as sounding like air slowly being released from a balloon, wasn't taking the hint.

"You know the other day when Ms. Martínez was talking about 'The Wizard of Oz'?" Myra droned on. "Well, I really do have the DVD. And it's not just the regular DVD, either. It's a special Collector's Edition. It's got lots of cool, behind-the-scenes stuff, including a clip of the jitterbug dance that was cut from the film. The producers felt that leaving the dance number in the movie might date it."

Thankfully, the line had shrunk. Raquel entered the serving area. "Good morning," she greeted the servers. "Everything looks so delicious today."

Normally, she didn't give the servers the time of day, but she needed to try something, anything, to silence the chatterbox.

The servers, unaccustomed to such a friendly reception, merely grunted as they piled scoops of food onto her tray.

"Did you know that Judy Garland wasn't the original choice to play Dorothy in 'The Wizard of Oz'?" Myra said. She wrapped some loose strands of her wiry, blond hair around her ears. "It was Shirley Temple. I think Shirley Temple would've made an even better Dorothy, don't you? Anyway, there was a contract dispute or something, so the studio decided to go with Judy Garland. Also, did you know that in the book, *The Wizard of Oz*, Dorothy had silver slippers, not ruby ones? I guess the moviemakers thought red would look better than silver on the screen."

Raquel paid for her food. She looked for a place to sit, but there were no empty chairs at any of her friends' tables.

Marco glanced up at her, and for a second they locked eyes. Raquel quickly turned away. Then, with almost no emotion in her voice, she asked Myra, "Would you like to sit with me?"

A wide, happy smile spread across Myra's face. "Sure!"

They found a table with two empty seats. After they sat down, Myra continued cranking out every piece of "Wizard of Oz" trivia she knew. That was fine. Raquel didn't care. As long as she didn't have to sit with Marco Díaz.

That sellout.

That's what she called him. A sellout. Plus a few choice cuss words in Spanish.

"You know that actor, Buddy Ebsen, who played Jed Clampett on the old 'Beverly Hillbillies' TV show?" Myra asked. "Did you know he was the original choice to play the Tin Man? Well, after they applied the makeup on him, he had a terrible reaction to the silver paint. It made him so sick he wound up in the hospital. That's why he had to give up his part in the movie."

Raquel watched Marco and his friends get up from their table. They dropped their trays off in the dishwashing area and went outside.

Raquel rose and grabbed her tray. "See you, Myra. I've got to go."

"Are you finished already?" Myra, who hadn't even touched her food, was disappointed her audience was leaving.

"Yeah. See you."

Raquel rushed off before the walking, talking, "Wizard of Oz" encyclopedia could say anything else.

She dumped her tray off, dashed out of the cafeteria, and headed down the hallway to the bathroom. Luckily, it was empty. Raquel entered a stall and sat on the toilet.

Her palms were clammy. Streaks of sweat trickled down her armpits, though the bathroom wasn't particularly hot. Her insides felt as if a ghostly hand had clutched her intestines and was refusing to let go.

When she went to the Alamo rehearsal yesterday, her intention was to apologize to Marco. She was even going to ask him to give her back the teddy bear. She would act so grateful to have it. Even if the bear did creep her out. Then she would invite him to walk home with her.

But things didn't work out that way.

As she watched Marco onstage in a scene with Moe Craddock, she became concerned about him. Marco looked exhausted. He sounded as if he was sick or something.

When the rehearsal was over, she asked him, "You feeling okay?"

"Sure, why?"

"You don't look well. And the way you were coughing while you were onstage, you sounded terrible."

Marco's face turned red. "Look, Raquel, I don't need for you to make fun of my acting. I'm doing the best I can. I'm not a professional, you know."

She winced. "I wasn't making fun of you, Marco. It's just . . ."

"It's real easy to criticize others when you don't have the guts to get up onstage, isn't it!" he snapped. He'd had enough of Raquel's constant whining. She didn't like the play, she didn't like his Valentine present and now she was making fun of his acting.

Raquel gritted her teeth. "You still don't get it, do you?"

"I get it just fine, Raquel! You're the one who doesn't get it. You know the saying: 'America, love it or leave it'? Well, if you don't like the way things are done here, why don't you go back to Mexico? I'm a proud Texan and a proud American!"

"No, I'll tell you what you are!" Raquel fired back. "You're a sellout!"

"What?"

"Yeah, that's right. Just like those Tejanos at the Alamo. And Lorenzo de Zavala. You think you're Jim Bowie who has to save Texas from us big bad Mexicans." Her voice degenerated to a guttural rasp. "Well, take a close look at your skin, Marco. It's as dark as mine." Then she unleashed a flood of cuss words that silenced the entire auditorium.

Raquel used the bathroom. Then she washed her hands and face. As she stepped into the hall, she heard voices coming from the teacher's workroom. The door was open, so she stole a peek. She saw Ms. Martínez talking to Mr. Watts. She looked as if she was crying.

What was wrong? Raquel liked her new teacher. She felt more welcomed in her room than she ever did with any of her other teachers. And she spoke Spanish.

"*La persona que sabe dos idiomas vale más.* The person who knows two languages is worth more," Ms. Martínez was fond of saying.

Another thing Raquel liked about her was that even though she was an English teacher, she stocked her shelves with lots of Spanish-language books. Raquel had borrowed a poetry book from her called *Yo soy amigo del pueblo y me gusta la canción.* Her teacher had recommended it. "I think you'll like it. It's one of my favorites."

Raquel wasn't into poetry, but she was enjoying this book. The poems in it made sense to her.

A disturbing thought, however, crossed her mind. If Ms. Martínez was so proud of her culture, why hadn't she spoken up about the Alamo play? Surely she had to see how offensive it was. Was Ms. Martínez a sellout, too?

The thought made Raquel shiver.

CHAPTER TWENTY-SIX

The Jesse Chisholm Coliseum, a dilapidated, dome-shaped structure, sat on the outskirts of downtown. It had originally been built to host rodeo events. Later, it became a venue for country and western concerts. Hank Williams had performed there. Patsy Cline, Carl Perkins, Johnny Cash, and Elvis Presley had all made appearances at the Jesse Chisholm Coliseum.

In recent years, however, it had become home for a small, independent, wrestling promotion called Star Spangled Wrestling.

It was also the site of the annual Golden Gloves Tournament. The coliseum had a seating capacity of almost 3,000. Tonight, it was sprinkled with about two hundred paying customers.

The old man led Marco Díaz up the ramp from the underground dressing rooms. Walking behind them was Angel Ramos, the owner of the East Grand Boxing Club. He would serve as Marco's second in the ring.

Marco was dressed in blue-and-white trunks with a matching blue-and-white jersey. Red gloves, sporting the familiar EVERLAST logo, covered his hands.

His opponent was A.C. Townsend, a tall, sinewy, light-skinned, African-American kid with a shaved head. Marco had fought him on three different occasions, coming out on top twice. The last time they fought was when Marco scored the first knockout of his career.

128

Their rematch tonight was the eighth one scheduled on a card that featured twenty-two fights. Boxers of all ages, sizes, and weights were clustered near ringside. They represented various boxing clubs, all under the supervision of the Amateur Athletic Union.

"You beat Townsend one more time, and we'll be back next month for the Texas state tournament," the old man reminded Marco.

But Marco's mind was not on tonight's fight, much less the state tournament. He still couldn't believe the argument he'd had with his girlfriend.

Girlfriend? Is that what Raquel was? His girlfriend? He'd never even kissed her, though he'd thought about it plenty of times. Marco had never had a girlfriend. There was Belinda Fuentes, a girl he had a crush on last year, but she moved away before anything happened between them.

He liked Raquel. He liked her a lot. But he didn't know how she felt about him. Sure, they hugged on occasion, but Raquel hugged everybody.

He'd thought about asking her out, maybe go to the show or something. But after the argument they had, he didn't know if she'd ever want to talk to him again.

You're a sellout, Marco.

He wasn't exactly sure what Raquel meant by that. But her words stung him nonetheless. He'd just wanted to be in the Alamo program. Playing Jim Bowie was fun. He was going to get to wear a costume and carry a knife and everything. He was even going to "die" onstage. Marco and Izzy had practiced how they'd fall down after they got shot.

You're a sellout, Marco.

He stood in the gold corner and shadowboxed to loosen his arms.

"Remember, stick to body shots," the old man advised. "Townsend's a big kid, but he's got a soft belly. That's how you beat him the last time. Work his stomach."

"I will, Grandpa," Marco promised.

A.C. Townsend, representing the Palomino Boxing Club, climbed through the ropes with his trainers. He stood in the green corner. He wore black-and-silver trunks and a matching jersey.

Marco noticed that A.C.'s arms had grown considerably muscular since the last time they'd fought. A.C. had probably been lifting weights. That didn't concern Marco too much. His grandfather didn't believe in lifting weights as part of the training.

"Weightlifting makes you muscle-bound," the old man had repeatedly cautioned. "It tightens your body, and you lose flexibility in your arms."

The ring announcer introduced them, with both boxers receiving an equal amount of applause from the sparse, but enthusiastic crowd. The referee called them to the center of the ring, where he gave them their final instructions. Then they returned to their respective corners.

At the sound of the bell, A.C. rushed out. Before Marco could get set, he was driven back with a solid right punch to his cheek. A quick left to his eye followed. Marco covered up, but A.C. attacked him with a flurry of punching combinations, lifting the crowd to its feet.

"Go to the body! Go to the body!" the old man screamed from outside the ring, his fists balled up, flailing the air.

A.C. continued the assault throughout the round.

Jab! Jab! Punch! Jab! Jab! Punch!

Finally, with about thirty seconds left, Marco connected with some telling shots to the body. A.C. winced and yelped in pain.

When the bell rang, Marco tottered to his corner and slumped on his stool. Angel Ramos squirted water into Marco's mouth and on his face.

"That was his round," the old man said. "You gave 'im a freebie. Next time, don't let 'im get the first jump. Remember, body shots. *¡A la panza, y con ganas!*"

In round two, Marco tried to go to the body, but A.C. kept him at bay with stinging jabs, causing him to hesitate with his punches. Marco realized he was being out-pointed. He swung desperately with a wide left hook that missed. He paid for it when A.C. snuck in a strong right cross that busted Marco's nose. Marco tasted his blood as it seeped into his mouth. The round came to an inglorious end with A.C. Townsend dancing in his corner.

Marco, sapped of energy and confidence, sank in his stool as Angel Ramos worked to stop the bleeding.

"You got 'im going, Marco!" the old man said, trying to sound optimistic. "He's getting tired. He's ready to be taken."

But Marco knew better. He was losing the fight. A.C. Townsend was too strong. Marco's jaw throbbed. He thought he had a loose tooth.

"Work the body!" the old man shouted as the bell rang for the third and final round.

Marco stood in the middle of the ring and waited for A.C. to come to him. If he was going to win the fight, he had to stop A.C. now. Marco bit hard on his mouthpiece. He started with three quick jabs to A.C.'s face. As A.C. raised his arms to block a fourth one, Marco drove his fist into A.C.'s stomach. He landed another punch. Then another. And another.

"That's it, Marco!" the old man shrieked. "Hit 'im!"

A.C. doubled over, wrapping his arms around his stomach. This gave Marco the opening he needed. He whacked him on the head with rapid-fire rights and lefts.

The frenzied crowd rose to its feet, screaming and cheering.

"Finish him, Marco!" the old man yelled. "Finish him! He's yours!"

A.C. grabbed Marco in a bear hug, preventing him from throwing any more punches. The referee pulled them apart. Then he warned A.C. about clinching.

A fast right hook by Marco caught A.C. on the jaw, but A.C. fired back with a steady stream of punches. They no longer had the effect they did in round one, but they were still accumulating points.

The final round ended with both fighters trading wild, out of control punches.

The appreciative audience gave them a loud, standing ovation.

"You did good out there, Marco," the old man said. "I told you Townsend had a soft belly."

Marco was relieved that he had finally worked his grandfather's strategy. But was it enough to win the fight? A.C. was tougher than he'd ever been in the past.

While the ring announcer collected the ballots from the judges at ringside, the referee stood in the center of the ring, holding Marco and A.C.'s arms.

"The winner by decision," the announcer said in a deep voice, " . . . A.C. Townsennnd!"

The referee raised A.C.'s arm in victory. Applause rang out for both boxers.

A.C. turned and hugged Marco. "Good fight, man."

"Yeah, thanks."

Marco stepped out of the ring, dejected.

His grandfather patted him on the back. "Don't let it get you down, boy. You did the best you could. That's all I asked for. You were busier in there than a one-legged man in a butt-kicking contest."

Marco faked a smile. His nose started to bleed again. It was probably broken. His jaw felt as if it had been hit with a brick. His right eye was beginning to shut.

That was it. Marco was through for the year. He wouldn't return for the state tournament next month. All that training, all that hard work, all that advice, it was all for nothing.

He hung his head as he dragged himself back to the dressing room. In one day, he'd managed to lose his girl-friend, his boxing match, and, he was beginning to believe, his self-respect.

CHAPTER TWENTY-SEVEN

Mrs. Frymire stood at the center of the stage. "Let me have your attention!"

Buzz. Buzz. Buzz.

"Let me have your attention!"

Buzz. Buzz. Buzz.

Mrs. Pruitt stood up. "If you kids don't settle down, we're going to put a stop to this right now and send everyone home! Do you understand?"

Buzz. Buzz. Buzz.

"DO YOU UNDERSTAND?"

The auditorium fell silent.

"Raise your hand if you signed up to be a dancer," Mrs. Frymire said.

A number of hands went up.

"I'm sorry, but I'm afraid we will no longer have dancers in the show," she told the group. Her voice sounded strained. "However, if you are still interested in being in the program, please see Mr. Gewertz and let him know that you will now be part of the choir."

"What happened?" Norma Herrera asked. "Why aren't we having the dances?"

Mrs. Frymire sighed. "Ms. Martínez is no longer involved with the show."

"Why not?"

"It was her decision," Mrs. Frymire said. She didn't offer any more information. "All right, let's go ahead and get started." She opened her black binder.

"What do you mean, *it was her decision?*" Arlene Furr questioned. "Why did Ms. Martínez quit?"

Mrs. Pruitt stood up. "We need to get on with the rehearsal, or we'll be here all night."

Mrs. Frymire ignored Arlene's question. She called Herb Williams to the stage, and she told Allen Gray to take his place at the top of the aisle. "When I give you the signal, Allen, run up to the stage and say your lines, okay? Go!"

Allen slowly trotted down the aisle.

"Faster!" Mrs. Frymire cried. "The way you've always done it."

Allen picked up the pace, but it was still a lackluster run. "Colonel. Colonel Travis. They're coming after us. Hurry." Allen was unable to infuse the slightest bit of enthusiasm into his voice. In addition to having a small speaking part, he was also supposed to dance with Arlene in the "Cotton-Eyed Joe" number. He'd been looking forward to dancing with her. But now the dance was cut.

Herb: "Whoa there, son. Calm down. What's the problem?"

Allen, in an unemotional voice: "The Mexican Army's heading toward Texas. I've gotta warn Colonel Travis."

Herb: "The Colonel already knows about that. In fact, we just finished a meeting to make plans on how we're gonna fight 'em."

Allen: "We're gonna fight Santa Anna's army?"

"Say it with more feeling, Allen," Mrs. Frymire urged.

But Allen didn't feel like saying it with more feeling. He was wondering why Ms. Martínez was no longer teaching the dances. What happened?

Herb: "I don't think we've got a choice."

Allen: "But where are we gonna fight an army that big?"

Herb: "There's only one logical place. The Alamo!"

Allen: "The Alamo."

"No, Allen, you're not making a statement," Mrs. Frymire said. "You're asking a question. Make your voice go higher."

Allen repeated: "The Alamo."

"Allen, you've done this a million times," Mrs. Frymire said with exasperation in her voice. "Say it in the form of a question. Say, 'The Alamo?'"

Allen: "The Alamo?"

"That's it. Herb, finish it."

Herb: "That's right. The Alamo."

"Good."

Marco Díaz sat by himself in the back row of the auditorium. Throughout the day, he had avoided his classmates as much as possible. His jaw was swollen, his lip was cut, and a black welt had blossomed below his right eye.

He had wanted to stay home from school. His parents told him he could, but his grandfather talked him out of it.

"You can't hide every time you lose, Marco. In life, like in boxing, you got your wins and your losses. Remember that. And as far as your bruises and cuts are concerned, they're a badge of courage. It shows you got the guts to step in the ring and fight. You think Evander Holyfield hid his ear when Mike Tyson bit a chunk of it? 'Course not. He showed it off! And you know why? 'Cause it was his badge of courage. Now go to school, and don't think about your face."

Marco had expected Raquel to ask him about his bruises, to check if he was all right, but she'd been ignoring him all day.

Billy Ray, Luther, Andy, and Agatha took the stage.

Billy Ray: "Williams! Check the supply room. I want a full count of every weapon available."

Luther: "Yes sir, Colonel Travis."

There was a pause.

"Agatha?" Mrs. Frymire called.

"Oops, sorry." She straightened her bangs. "You really believe they're coming, don't you?"

Billy Ray: "They're coming, all right. I just got word that Santa Anna was seen crossing the Rio Grande. He'll be here before we know it."

Agatha: "Four or five thousand men?"

"No, Agatha," Mrs. Frymire said. "That's Andy's line. You're supposed to say, 'How many soldiers do you figure he'll bring with him, Colonel?'"

Agatha blushed. "Sorry. How many soldiers do you figure he'll bring with him?'"

"Colonel."

"Colonel."

Billy Ray: "As mad as he is with us right now, I expect he'll have around four or five thousand men."

Andy: "Four or five thousand men? Colonel, we don't have enough volunteers to fight an army that big!"

Another pause.

"Agatha?"

Agatha peered about, wild-eyed. She dug her nails into her palms.

"Agatha?"

"Can you please give me the first couple of words?"

Mrs. Frymire frowned. "I'll tell you what. Let me work with another group. In the meantime, why don't you sit in the back and read over your lines?"

Billy Ray scowled at Agatha. Then he leaned into her and whispered something in her ear that made her reel in shock.

Mrs. Frymire thumbed through the script. "Okay, let's go over the next scene." She called the performers onstage.

Marco trudged up to the stage and joined the others.

"We'll play some music here, an interlude," Mrs. Frymire explained, "to give everyone a chance to set up. As soon as the music is over, Marco will start."

Marco lowered his head. He was embarrassed to have the stage lights shining on his face, exposing his bruises. But more than that, he was embarrassed to be onstage playing Jim Bowie.

"Marco? Are you ready?"

He shrugged. "Sure." He faced Billy Ray, and in a slow, unemotional voice said, "The Alamo's been secured, Travis. It's about as ready as it's gonna be."

In past rehearsals, he had coughed after this line. But Marco didn't feel like fake coughing anymore. He wanted to be done with the scene and get off the stage.

Billy Ray: "Have we heard anything from Colonel Fannin? I understand he's got about a thousand men in Goliad."

Herb: "Are you sure about that? I heard that Fannin had less than four hundred soldiers."

Billy Ray: "Well, we aren't gonna tell the men that. As far as they're concerned, we've got a thousand reinforcements coming."

Marco: "I guess it doesn't matter how many men we've got. Santa Anna's still coming. That's the one thing we can be sure of. El Presidente's on his way."

"Good," Mrs. Frymire said. "All right, let's skip to Scene Eleven."

As the boys stepped down from the stage, Mrs. Frymire stopped Marco. "Would you read Izzy's part for now? I'm still trying to find someone to take his place."

Myra Coonrod's hand shot up in the air. "Mrs. Frymire! Mrs. Frymire! I can take Izzy's place."

The teacher ignored her.

Marco took the script and read: "De time has come. We weel make plans to attack de Alamo for de las' time." The words made him cringe. He was almost glad he and Raquel had had that argument. At least she wasn't sitting in the auditorium listening to him.

Orlando: "Pardon me, bot wooden eet be better to wait onteel Gómez arrives weeth de beeg cannons?"

Marco: "Why wait? Messanchers go een an' out of de Alamo like flies. Jesterday, teddy-two solchers from Gonzales arrived. Chall we wait onteel dey get stronger? No."

"Keep going, Marco."

"Eet ees time to en' dees rebellion. We chall attack een de morning."

"Excellent!" Mrs. Frymire said. "All right, let's get ready for the battle scene."

Mr. Watts, who had been placed in charge of choreographing the fight scenes, called the Texan and the Mexican soldiers to the front. "Remember, each of you has been assigned a soldier to shoot. When you're shot, just go down naturally. Don't exaggerate your fall. After all, we're not handing out Academy Awards for best performances."

The kids laughed.

"Pretend you're holding rifles and make exploding noises with your mouths as you attack. Next week, Ms. Posey will help you make the rifles you'll use in the play." He turned to the music teacher and formed an "okay" signal with his thumb and forefinger. Mr. Gewertz nodded, then turned on the CD player. Trumpet music sounded.

John Ahne as soldier Number One: "What is it? What's going on?"

Eric Walker as soldier Number Two: "They're playing 'El Degüello,' the death song. I guess this is it, old buddy. They're coming after us for sure. Well, if we don't make it here, I'll meet ya at the pearly gates."

Billy Ray as William B. Travis thrust his plastic sword in the air. "If this is to be our final battle, let's show 'em what Texans are made of. In the name of liberty . . . attack!"

Mexican soldiers ran down the aisles of the auditorium holding their arms out in firing positions.

This was the part Marco had been waiting for, the grand finale, the biggest battle scene in the play. But his heart was no longer in it. He plodded across the stage like a tired circus elephant.

"Ploosh!"

"Blam!"

"Pow! Pow!"

"*¡Viva México!*" Felipe shouted.

"*¡Viva Santa Anna!*" Orlando ad-libbed. He'd heard a Mexican soldier shout it in a documentary Mrs. Pruitt had shown them about the Alamo, and he thought it sounded cool.

One by one, Texans and Mexicans dropped to the floor.

Herb Williams, Allen Gray, John Ahne, Eric Walker, as well as Henry Torres, Alberto Castro, and José Montes fell. Marco halfheartedly got down on one knee and lay down beside them.

Orlando Chávez aimed his imaginary rifle at Billy Ray Cansler.

"Pow!"

But Billy Ray refused to go down.

"Pow! Pow!"

Still Billy Ray refused to "die." He didn't want to be "killed" by a weenie like Orlando Chávez.

"Drop to the floor, Billy Ray!" Mr. Watts ordered.

Billy Ray ignored him. He continued waving his plastic sword in the air, leading his army onward, even though all the Texans were "dead."

Finally, Marco reached up and yanked Billy Ray by the waist of his loose trousers. His pants slipped down below his knees.

"Hey!" Billy Ray instantly dropped to the floor and scrambled around as he tried to pull his pants back up.

The kids, even the "dead" ones, howled with laughter.

Marco Díaz sat up. "Well, what do you know? You do wear Pampers after all."

Red-faced and wild-eyed, Billy Ray ran behind the curtain and pulled up his pants.

"Marco!" Mrs. Pruitt screeched. "Go to the office right now! That was completely unacceptable. I'm filling out a referral."

"Go ahead," Marco muttered. "I've had it with this. I quit!" He walked out of the auditorium.

Myra Coonrod's hand went up. "Mrs. Frymire! Mrs. Frymire! Can I take Marco's place?"

The teacher's face crumpled. She knew exactly how Marco felt. At that moment, she felt like quitting, too.

Backstage, Billy Ray could hear the kids in the audience still laughing their heads off. *I'm gonna get 'im. He's gonna pay for this.*

But how? Where?

His father had warned him about what Mr. Rathburn had said after Izzy got hurt. "That principal's looking for a reason to kick you out of school, son. Don't give 'im one."

Billy Ray also recalled his father telling him the reason Mr. Rathburn couldn't do anything about what happened to Izzy was because it happened away from school. *He's gonna be so sorry he ever decided to mess with me. And I know just how I'll do it.*

CHAPTER TWENTY-EIGHT

"We need to make a decision now," Mrs. Frymire told her colleagues. They had gathered in her science lab to discuss their crisis. Ms. Martínez was not invited to join them. "Mr. Cansler is scheduled to be here on Saturday morning to build the Alamo for us. The question is, are we still putting on the play?"

Mr. Watts fidgeted with a plastic model of the human body that was sitting on the table. "I don't see how we can. Izzy's out, Marco's out, and Orlando and Felipe told me this morning they don't want to be in the play either."

"Allen's out, too," Mrs. Pruitt said. "Now, Billy Ray's threatening to quit. He says he doesn't want to get back onstage after the way Marco embarrassed him."

Mrs. Frymire sighed. "We don't have costumes. Izzy's mother has refused to make them for us. Sandy has quit. And, since we cut out the dance numbers, the dancers are mad. A lot of our girls have dropped out of the choir."

"Maybe we should postpone it until later," Mrs. Pruitt suggested.

Mr. Watts pulled the liver out of the model, causing the rest of the body parts to fall out. He grinned sheepishly. "Sorry." He tried to place the pieces back in the body, but he couldn't get them to fit. "I hate to say I told you so, Doris, but . . . " He shrugged. "I told you so. Putting on a play's not as easy as it looks. I don't know how Miss Mac managed to do it year after year."

Mrs. Frymire gazed out the window. Her eyes welled with tears. This play was supposed to be a tribute to her beloved friend. Instead, it had turned out to be a disaster. Her throat became constricted. *I'm sorry, Miss Mac,* she thought.

She turned to her colleagues and said, "I guess we'll just have to tell Mr. Cansler we're not doing it."

CHAPTER TWENTY-NINE

Light snow had fallen throughout the day. Now, the precipitation had picked up, filling the air with large-sized snowflakes.

Marco Díaz stood on the second story of the building frame and waited. A frosty breeze blew on his face. He hoped his plan would work. If it didn't, he was dead meat. He saw someone bundled up in a hooded, navy blue coat walking toward the construction site.

It's not him, he thought. *He wouldn't dare come by himself.*

A few seconds later, Raquel Flores approached the building. She cupped her hands around her mouth. "Marco, can I talk to you?"

He scanned the area to make sure no one else was coming. Then he jumped off, landing on the snow-covered sand pile.

"Where's Izzy?" she asked.

Marco dusted off his pants. "He doesn't want to hang out here anymore. Not since his accident."

Raquel gazed up at the towering steel structure. "I don't blame him."

They took a stroll around the construction site. Marco kept glancing behind his shoulder as they walked.

"How did your boxing match go? Did you win?"

Marco stuck out his chin. "Look at my face. Does it look like I won?"

"Sorry."

"That's okay. I'm not sure I really want to be a boxer, after all. Too much work."

The chilly February air swirled around them. Raquel bunched the collar of her coat around her neck. "I heard you quit the Alamo program."

He shrugged. "I was probably going to get kicked out of it anyway. Doesn't matter, though. The program's been cancelled." He gave her a sidelong glance. "I guess that ought to make you happy."

She furrowed her brows. Then a grin spread across her face. "I'll tell you what made me happy. It was hearing how you pulled Billy Ray's pants down in front of everybody." She giggled. "I wish I had been there when it happened."

He looked over his shoulder again. "Yeah, it was pretty funny. I guess it was worth the in-house suspension Mr. Rathburn gave me."

Her face became solemn. "That's not fair, Marco. I mean, Billy Ray almost kills Izzy, but Mr. Rathburn doesn't do anything to him. All you do is embarrass Billy Ray, and you get a suspension."

Marco thought he glimpsed movement behind a tree. He kept his eyes focused on that spot for a moment, but he didn't see anyone.

Raquel looped her arm around his and leaned against him. "Marco, I'm sorry for the awful things I said to you the other day. Please forgive me."

"No, that's okay. You were right. I *am* a sellout."

"No, you're not. I was wrong to call you that." She searched for the right words. She didn't want to say anything that might cause another blow up. "You were standing up for your country, Marco. You're an American, and you should be proud of that." She paused. "But I hope you understand that as proud as you are of being an American, I'm just as proud to be a *mexicana.*" She swallowed a lump that had formed in her throat. "It's just that in Mexico, we're taught that the Texans were the enemy. They were rebels who had no respect for our laws. I know they're considered great heroes here, but that's not the way they're seen in Mexico." She drew in a deep breath. "But like you said, that's my truth, not yours."

Marco mused over what she said. "I guess sometimes there's more than one truth."

She pressed her cheek on his arm. It felt warm, comforting.

"I'm going to Izzy's," Marco said. "Wanna come?"

"Sure. It's freezing out here."

"Here, let me warm you up." He wrapped his arm around her waist and pulled her close.

She turned and faced him. Then she reached up, clasped his face in her hands, and kissed him on the lips. She'd never kissed a boy before, so she didn't know if she was doing it right.

Marco squeezed her tightly. He closed his eyes as he enjoyed the softness of her lips against his. He had waited a long time for this moment.

"Enjoying yourself, lover boy?"

Marco spun around.

Billy Ray was standing behind him. And as Marco had predicted, Billy Ray had not come alone.

CHAPTER THIRTY

Luther Bowers and Jacob and Joshua Bukowski stood at Billy Ray's side. So did two eighth-grade boys whose names Marco didn't know. He'd seen Billy Ray hang out with them from time to time. Though he didn't want to fight him, Marco realized that standing up to Billy Ray was the only way to end his and Izzy's problems with him. That was why he had accepted his challenge.

Billy Ray sneered at him with the confidence of someone who has the advantage of six guys against one. "You been begging for a fight for a long time, Marco." He spread out his arms. "Well, here I am. Come get some."

Raquel scoffed at him. "You sound real tough for a guy who wears girls' underwear. Everybody saw your panties when Marco pulled your pants down."

Billy Ray's gang snickered.

He whipped around and glowered at them. Then he aimed a finger at her. "You'd better shut up, Raquel. I don't like to hit girls, but . . ."

"Leave her alone!" Marco growled.

Billy Ray stared defiantly at him. "What are you gonna do about it, punk?"

Marco didn't respond. Instead, he took a step back.

With a satisfied smirk on his face, Billy Ray said, "That's what I thought." He inched closer, but Marco continued to back away. "Come on, punk," Billy Ray taunted.

He motioned for Marco to come to him. "Show your girl-friend what a tough guy you are."

Marco continued walking backwards. Then as Billy Ray closed in, he took off running.

Billy Ray chortled. "Look at him. He's a coward. He says he's a Golden Gloves boxer, but he probably got beaten up by a five-year-old girl."

Billy Ray's gang gave chase. Marco headed for the steel structure. Before they could catch him, he shinnied up to the second floor.

"Leave him alone!" Raquel cried. "It's not fair. It's six against one!"

Billy Ray laughed. "Yeah, six against one. Hey, just like it was at the Alamo. Well, now it's our turn. Remember the Alamo!"

He scooped a handful of snow and shaped it into a ball. *I'll knock the coward down just like I did to Izzy.*

Whzzz!

The snowball sailed about three feet away from Marco.

Luther, the Bukowski brothers, and the two eighth graders followed Billy Ray's lead.

Whzzz! Whzzz! Whzzz! Whzzz! Whzzz!

"Remember the Alamo!" they shouted.

They missed each time. Marco ducked behind a gird-er to avoid getting hit. He gathered some snow from the beam he was standing on and made a large ball.

Whzzz, whap!

Bingo! He tagged Billy Ray on the face.

Whzzz! Whzzz! Whzzz!

Marco dodged each snowball thrown at him.

Whzzz, whap! Whzzz, whap! Whzzz, whap!

Marco connected with almost every shot. Out in the open, with nothing to hide behind, Billy Ray and his gang were easy targets.

Whzzz, whap! Whzzz, whap! Whzzz, whap!

The snowballs didn't hurt, but Billy Ray was furious that he was getting pelted each time.

"Knock 'im down from there!" he hollered, pointing an angry finger up at Marco. "Remember the Alamo!"

The Bukowskis and Luther Bowers started to climb up the building structure. "Remember the Alamo!"

The two eighth graders, not accustomed to being given orders by a seventh grader, stood back and watched.

Marco disappeared behind a girder. He came back out, dragging a five-gallon plastic container. It was filled with slushy, cold water.

"Remember the Alamo!" Billy Ray's gang shouted.

"Remember who won!" Marco yelled back. He poured the freezing water on Luther and the Bukowskis.

Splash!

Billy Ray's gang spluttered. They shivered. They shook. But they clung to the girder like cats stuck on a tree.

Marco dragged out a second plastic container.

Splash!

Drenched with the unforgiving frigid coldness of the water, Luther and the Bukowskis finally let go of the girder. They fell, hitting the snowy ground with a thud.

Raquel hooted with laughter. So did Billy Ray's eighth-grade friends.

"I . . . I . . . I'm freezing!" Luther wailed, rubbing his arms.

"I . . . It's c . . . cold!" Joshua and Jacob Bukowski cried. Their teeth chattered like castanets.

Marco brought out a third plastic container. When Billy Ray's gang saw it, their eyes widened with fear.

They scrammed out of the construction site, abandoning their leader. They were desperate to get out of their soaking wet clothes.

The eighth graders, deciding the fight was over, left, too.

"Hey! Come back here!" Billy Ray hollered. But no one listened to him.

Marco climbed down from the building.

The blood drained from Billy Ray's face. He held his hands up in surrender and backed away. "I . . . I don't want to fight you, Marco."

"Funny, you sure did a minute ago," Marco said.

"You're not so tough now, are you?" Raquel said scornfully.

Marco growled at Billy Ray. "I told you to leave Izzy alone. But you wouldn't listen, would you?"

Billy Ray's face became ashen. His legs trembled uncontrollably. His heart pounded wildly in his chest. "Wh . . . what are you g . . . gonna do?"

Marco balled his hand into a fist and shoved it against Billy Ray's chin. "Now, listen, and listen good. I'm going to warn you one more time. Stay away from my friends, and stay away from me. Or else."

Billy Ray bobbed his head up and down.

"Good. Now get out of here."

Billy Ray didn't wait to be told twice. He scurried out of the construction site as fast as the snow- and ice-covered ground would let him.

After he was gone, Raquel threw her arms around Marco's neck and declared, "That's the coolest thing I've ever seen. You're *my* hero!"

Marco smiled. He pulled her close. "Now, let's see. Where were we?"

CHAPTER THIRTY-ONE

"Don't open the door!" Marco and Raquel heard Blanca scream from inside the house. They looked at each other, puzzled. Marco tried the doorbell again.

This time Izzy opened the door and let them in.

"Shut the door! Shut the door! Don't let the cabbit get out!"

Blanca was frenzied. She chased the white, terrified creature around the living room. It flew onto the sofa. Then it leaped on an end table. Blanca tried to reach for it, but the animal hopped off, sending the end table lamp crashing to the floor. The animal scampered out of the living room and disappeared into the kitchen.

"Doggone it, Blanca!" Izzy hollered. "I told you to leave that nasty cat alone. You'd better get rid of it before it tears the whole house apart!"

Ignoring her brother, Blanca raced to the kitchen.

They could hear chairs falling as Blanca desperately tried to grab her prize.

"Blancaaa!"

"Hey," Marco said in a mild voice, "don't be so mean to your little sister."

"Are you kidding? She's going to destroy the house trying to catch that cat!"

"No, she won't. And try not to call it a cat. Blanca thinks it's a cabbit, so let her think that."

Izzy wrinkled his brows. Once again, Marco the hero was coming to the rescue. Izzy had seen him fight in the ring. Marco battered his opponents with vicious punches. Yet, he could be such a gentleman outside the ring.

A gentleman. That's what Izzy was lacking. How to be a gentleman. He admired Marco and often wished he could be more like him. He used to think he wanted to possess Marco's fighting skills. He still did. But he realized what he needed more than that was how to be a gentleman. A gentle man.

Izzy calmed himself down. Then he said, "Blanca? Come here. I want to talk to you about the . . . cabbit."

Blanca poked her head from the kitchen. "Yeah?"

"If you want to catch the cabbit, why don't you pour some milk in a bowl and set it on the floor. See if it'll go to it?"

Blanca's face brightened. "Yeah. Good idea. And I'll lay out a carrot, too, in case he'd rather have that." She served the milk and the carrot and waited. After a little while, the long-eared animal came out from its hiding place under the breakfast table. It cautiously made its way toward the bowl. While it sipped the milk, Blanca stroked its back.

"That is one weird-looking cat," Izzy said. Marco elbowed him hard. "I . . . I mean, I've never seen a cabbit up close."

Blanca said, "I'm going to name it Cabby. What do you think?"

"It's perfect," Marco said.

Blanca picked up the carrot and offered it to the animal. It sniffed it for a second, then returned to the milk.

Izzy led Raquel and Marco back to the living room. "It's a cat. You know that, don't you?"

"Yes," Marco confessed. "But you don't need to tell Blanca that. It's a cabbit as far as I'm concerned."

Izzy smiled. "Like I said, that is one weird-looking cat."

"How's your head?" Raquel asked.

Izzy pressed his hand against the bandage. "Okay, I guess. I'm going back to school tomorrow. Except that . . . " He made a pained expression. "I'm kind of scared of Billy Ray. I don't know what he'll do when he sees me."

Marco patted him on the back. "He won't do anything to you, Iz. I promise."

"I guarantee you he won't," Raquel added with a smile.

Izzy shuddered. "I'll never mess with him again. That guy's crazy." He studied Marco's face. "Man, what did A.C. Townsend hit you with? A sledgehammer?"

Marco rubbed his jaw. "It felt like it."

Izzy looked closer. "What's the matter with your lip? Are you bleeding or something?"

Raquel blushed and covered her mouth.

Marco quickly wiped his lips with the back of his hand. "Uh, no. I, uh, had a red Popsicle on the way over here."

"In this freezing weather?" Izzy asked in disbelief. "Man, you must've really wanted to eat a Popsicle."

Wanting to change the subject, Raquel pointed to the blue taffeta fabric piled next to Izzy's mother's sewing machine. "What's all that?"

Izzy set the lamp the cat knocked down back on the end table. A piece of the lamp's base had chipped off. He turned the lamp around so the damage couldn't be seen at a glance. "That's what my mom was making our Alamo costumes out of. Here, let me show you."

He opened a hall closet and brought out a shiny blue shirt. It had gold epaulets sewn on each shoulder. Four brass buttons came down the front of the shirt.

"That is so cool," Marco said. He took it off the hanger and pressed it against his chest.

Izzy sighed. "Too bad my mom took me out of the program. Now she's mad 'cause it's been cancelled."

"Why should she care?" Raquel asked. "You're not in it."

Izzy took the shirt from Marco and placed it back on the hanger. "I know, but she spent a lot of money making the costumes. When I got hurt and she pulled me out of the program, she told the teachers she wasn't going to make the costumes. Then she realized that if she didn't finish them, she wouldn't get paid. She was going to let me be back in the show, but now it's been cancelled, so she's stuck with all these shirts."

"Can't she sell them to somebody?" Marco suggested.

Izzy smiled. "Sure." He held up the shirt. "Want to buy one?"

"What if we could talk the teachers into putting the play back on?" Raquel asked.

Marco's jaw dropped. He blinked in surprise. "What?"

"I know, I know. I'm guilty, Judge," she joked. "Look, I still don't care about the play, but I don't want Izzy's mom to have to lose all that money."

Marco stuck his hands in his pockets. He lowered his eyes and said, "I don't want Izzy's mom to lose her money either, but I don't want to be the one to talk to the teachers. I mean, I quit the show."

Izzy nodded. "I wouldn't know what to say either. Mrs. Frymire doesn't like me 'cause I don't understand half the stuff she teaches in science. And Mrs. Pruitt just plain gives me the heebie-jeebies."

"Maybe I'll say something to them, then," Raquel said, but there was a tinge of uncertainty in her voice. Mrs. Frymire had offered her a part in the play as a narrator, but she had turned it down. Ms. Martínez had invited her to be a dancer, but she had turned that down, too. How could she talk to the teachers about putting the play back on when she wasn't even willing to participate in it?

Blanca came out of the kitchen cradling the cat in her arms. She sat on the sofa and caressed its back. The cat purred contentedly.

"I think Cabby's sleepy," Izzy told his sister.

She looked up at him and smiled.

Izzy felt proud for not ridiculing his sister over the cat . . . the cabbit. Maybe he could learn how to be a gentle man after all.

"If the teachers do decide to put the play back on, will you be in it?" Raquel asked Marco.

"Nah, I don't think so."

She took him by the hand and gazed candidly at him. "Marco, listen to me. You're not a sellout." Her voice cracked. "I . . . I wish I'd never called you that. It was a terrible thing to say. Please, I want you to be in the play. You're great onstage."

Marco smiled appreciatively. It felt good to know she cared about him. "That's not it, Raquel. It's just that after everything that's happened between Billy Ray and Izzy and me, I don't want to be onstage with him and pretend that we're friends, fellow Texans, fighting side by side. Billy Ray's a king-sized jerk. If the teachers decide to do the show, they'll have to find someone else to play Jim Bowie."

"I don't have a choice," Izzy grumbled. "I have to be in it, but I really don't want to. I have the stupidest lines in the whole play."

Raquel gave him a hug. "Don't worry about it, Izzy. You'll be fine." Then she jokingly added, "Jew are hereby ordered to be een de play, meester, because jour mami needs de mohney."

They laughed.

"How about you, Raquel?" Marco asked. "Will you change your mind about being in it? I'm sure you could still be in a dance."

"No, Ms. Martínez is no longer helping with the dances," Raquel said. "Remember?"

"Oh, yeah. Well, you could be a singer in the choir, then."

"But you can't be a soldier," Izzy teased.

"I don't know. I'll have to think about it." She joined Blanca on the sofa and petted the cat.

Marco turned to Izzy and said, "She's something else. You know that?"

"Raquel?" Izzy nodded. "She's pretty cool. Kind of like having another sister."

Marco smiled. His eyes sparkled with delight. "That's not exactly the word I would use to describe her."

CHAPTER THIRTY-TWO

Ms. Martínez was sitting at her computer entering grades. Overall, she was pleased with what she had accomplished in her short time at Rosemont School. Most of her students had done quite well, though there were still a few whose grades weren't where they needed to be. But she was optimistic that she could help turn those students around before the school year was over.

Raquel poked her head inside the classroom and knocked. "Hi, you busy?"

Ms. Martínez glanced up. "*Hola, Raquel. Pasa.* What's up?"

"I came to return your book." She handed her *Yo soy amigo del pueblo y me gusta la canción.*

Ms. Martínez looked at the cover. On it was a drawing of a mariachi singer. He was playing his guitar on a street corner in a small village. A group of smiling peasants was gathered around him.

"Did you like it?"

"Yes. Some of the poems were silly, like the one called '*Accidente en una huevería.*'"

Ms. Martínez smiled in approval.

"But there was one that made me think about a problem Marco and I had. The one called '*Ilusión perdida.*'"

"*Pero últimamente, todo fue ilusión, ilusión perdida.* But ultimately, everything was an illusion, a lost illusion," Ms. Martínez recited from the poem.

"I made a copy of it," Raquel said. "I hope that's okay." She glanced around the empty room. "Do I have to go back to class?"

Ms. Martínez closed out her computer program. "Why? What class is it?"

"Art. But Ms. Posey's not here today. We've got that creepy substitute, the Pirate."

Ms. Martínez gave her a puzzled smile. "Who?"

"Mrs. Abernathy. The kids call her the Pirate. Do you know who she is?"

"No."

"Well, the Pirate is about this tall." Raquel raised her hand about four-feet high. "She has short gray hair and purple lips. She also wears prescription sunglasses. Except that one of the lenses from her glasses is missing, so she looks like she's wearing an eye patch. That's why we call her the Pirate."

"She sounds interesting," Ms. Martínez said.

"No, she's not. She's weird. Everybody has to be super quiet around her. She goes crazy if anybody makes any noise. She even sent Eric Walker to the office for sneezing."

"For sneezing?" Ms. Martínez chuckled. "Why did she do that?"

"She said Eric was disturbing the class. So can I stay?"

Ms. Martínez swiveled her chair around to face Raquel. "I don't know. What reason am I going to give her for you not returning to her classroom?"

Raquel took a seat across from her teacher. "I told her you needed the book right away, so she let me leave the room to bring it to you. Maybe you can tell her I had to finish writing a book report on it."

Ms. Martínez thumbed through the poetry book. She found *"Ilusión perdida"* and skimmed through it. "What happened between you and Marco? I thought you two were friends."

"We are." Raquel thought back to Marco's kiss. She could still feel a tingling sensation on her lips. "Ms. Martínez, if I tell you something, will you promise not to tell anybody?"

"Of course. My lips are sealed." She pretended to zip up her mouth.

Raquel sat back in her chair and placed her hands on her lap. She started by telling her teacher why she didn't want to be in the Alamo program. She felt she owed her an explanation. Ms. Martínez had pleaded with her to be in it, but Raquel had refused without giving her a reason. She also shared with her teacher how she had blown up in Texas history class. Ms. Martínez had already heard that story from Mrs. Pruitt. Raquel then told her about her argument with Marco and how she'd called him a sellout. That's why he'd quit the play. She even told her teacher about their kiss after they made up.

Ms. Martínez listened quietly without offering any comments or opinions.

Raquel talked about the confrontation at the construction site between Marco and Billy Ray and his gang. Ms. Martínez laughed when Raquel told her about how Marco had dumped cold water on Luther and the Bukowskis. She also explained that even though she had apologized to Marco, he didn't want to be Jim Bowie anymore because he didn't want to be on Billy Ray's side. Then she told her about how Izzy's mother was mad that the play had been cancelled because she had lost all that money from the unfinished costumes.

"Is there any chance you could put the play back on?" Raquel asked, finally.

Ms. Martínez looked at her uncomfortably. After all, she, too, had quit. "I don't know."

Raquel giggled nervously. "Izzy's mad because if you decide to do the play, he'll have to be in it. And he really hates his part."

"I don't blame him," Ms. Martínez said. She quickly glanced at her open door to make sure no one was listening. "He and Orlando and Felipe sounded terrible."

Raquel looked confused. "Then why didn't you tell Mrs. Frymire to change it?"

"What makes you so sure I didn't?"

"You did?" Raquel lowered her voice to a whisper. "What did she say?"

Ms. Martínez shrugged. "She said it was written that way to make the Mexicans sound . . . Mexicanish."

Raquel gazed down at the book she had just returned. "If she wanted to make the Mexicans sound Mexicanish, why didn't she just have them say their lines in Spanish?"

Ms. Martínez looked puzzled. Then her face brightened. *It could work!* If only she could get them to go along with it. She rose from her chair.

"Sorry, Raquel, but there's something I need to do."

Raquel groaned, "Where are you going?"

Ms. Martínez smiled. "To try to teach a horse how to fly."

CHAPTER THIRTY-THREE

Mrs. Frymire had a befuddled look on her face. "Spanish? Spanish?" she repeated, as if it was the most insane idea she'd ever heard. She shook her head as she paced the science lab floor. "Sandy, nobody will be able to understand what the kids are saying!"

"They won't necessarily have to. But when the audience sees the Mexican Army onstage, they'll figure the Mexicans are planning their attack on the Alamo, even if they don't understand Spanish."

Mr. Watts stopped playing with the model of the human body he had been taking apart. He set the plastic organs on the table. "Sandy, I think that is brilliant. Absolutely brilliant. Just think how authentic it'll sound."

"I also think we should add the character of Santa Anna to the play," Ms. Martínez continued. "After all, he is mentioned in the narration. Besides, the name Santa Anna sounds much better than Mexican Number One."

Mrs. Frymire mulled it over. "I don't know. I don't feel comfortable tampering with Miss Mac's play. I think we need to present it exactly the way she wrote it."

Mr. Watts snapped his fingers. "What about this? What if we call it 'Thirteen Days to Glory—The Battle of the Alamo,' based on the play written by Josephine McKeever? They do it all the time when movies are based on books."

"That's another thing," Ms. Martínez said. "I'd like to shorten the title." She knew she was pushing it, but as long as they were talking about the play without shouting at one another, she decided to air out all her ideas. "I think it should be called, 'The Battle of the Alamo.' Period."

Mrs. Frymire realized she had very little choice. If they were going to present Miss Mac's play at all, or a variation of it, she would have to give in. She turned to Mrs. Pruitt. "Claire?"

Mrs. Pruitt cleared her throat. "Well, as long as we're making changes, I want to throw this idea out in the open, see what you think. Raquel Flores mentioned something in my class the other day that's been gnawing at me ever since. What if somewhere in the play we add a couple of lines that show the Mexicans' perspective of the Alamo story?"

"What do you mean?" Mrs. Frymire worried that they might be deviating too far from Miss Mac's script.

"I'm not sure." Mrs. Pruitt rested her chin on her closed fist. "But times have changed since Miss Mac wrote that play. I don't know. Maybe it worked back then, but I have to agree with Sandy that the Mexicans' dialogue doesn't sound appropriate today."

Ms. Martínez breathed a silent sigh of relief. She couldn't believe that Mrs. Pruitt, of all people, was actually agreeing with her. "If it's all right with everyone, I'd be happy to write the Spanish dialogue. And I can include the changes Mrs. Pruitt suggested."

"That's fine with me," Mr. Watts said. "'Cause I sure can't do it. The only thing I remember from my high school Spanish class is *Mi mamá es bonita. Mi papá es buenos.*"

"I don't know about all this," Mrs. Frymire murmured. "I wonder what Miss Mac would think if she knew what we were doing to her play."

Mr. Watts held up the plastic heart from the human model. "Aw come on, Doris, have a heart."

She snatched the plastic heart out of his hand. "The Spanish part *would* give the play a unique flavor," she conceded. "And I've always thought the title was too long. And presenting Mexico's views on the Alamo would certainly make it more interesting." She looked at Ms. Martínez. "And you will help with the dances, won't you?"

"Of course. Honestly, I want this play to be a success as much as you do."

Mrs. Frymire smiled. "All right. Let's do it."

"Who will we get to play Santa Anna?" Mrs. Pruitt asked. "Felipe's too short, and Orlando's too skinny. And Izzy . . . " She didn't need to explain.

"I've got the perfect choice," Ms. Martínez said. "Marco Díaz."

"No can do," Mr. Watts said with a shake of his head. "He's playing Jim Bowie. Or at least, he was."

Ms. Martínez said, "I think he'll be much happier playing Santa Anna. I'll ask him."

Mrs. Frymire thought it over. "I suppose we can give Bowie to Luther Bowers. He doesn't have much of a speaking part, and he works well with Billy Ray."

"Too well," Mrs. Pruitt muttered under her breath.

"Marco Díaz as Santa Anna and Billy Ray Cansler as William B. Travis," Mr. Watts said. "That alone ought to be worth the price of admission."

CHAPTER THIRTY-FOUR

The front rows of the Josephine McKeever Memorial Auditorium were filled with noisy and excited students. Word had spread quickly that the Alamo program was back on. The kids had also learned that Ms. Martínez would teach the dances after all.

Earlier, she had spoken with Marco Díaz about accepting the role of Santa Anna. Marco was reluctant at first, but agreed to play the part when she explained that his dialogue would now be delivered in Spanish. He thought that would please Raquel. Also, he liked the idea of going up against Billy Ray Cansler's William B. Travis and defeating him at the Alamo.

Orlando Chávez and Felipe Garza, too, were thrilled to know that they were not going to have to talk in that phony accent. Izzy Peña was also glad to be back in it. As soon as he told his mom that the show was back on, she quickly called Mrs. Frymire and let her know that she would make the costumes and that she would allow her son to participate in the program.

While the other teachers helped the actors practice their lines, Ms. Martínez worked with the dancers. The Alamo included two dance numbers: "Cotton-Eyed Joe," a lively square dance, plus an original number Ms. Martínez created. She called it "The Widows' Dance." It was a slow, mournful dance performed to a song called *"El viaje misterioso."*

Unlike "Cotton-Eyed Joe," which involved boys and girls, "The Widows' Dance" featured girls only. It would come after the first attack.

Twelve girls stood in two rows facing the audience. As the music began, the girls pretended to hold the ends of their long skirts and swayed back and forth. Ms. Martínez told them they would be wearing black, flowing skirts with black tops. She had found the skirts among the many costumes Miss Mac had used in her programs over the years. The girls danced, moving forward then backward, with short, scissors-kick steps and turns.

Myra Coonrod had resigned herself to be a dancer, since she couldn't be a soldier. As she danced, she imagined herself in her black dress with her hair braided in red, white, and green ribbons. Ms. Martínez had promised the girls that she would fix their hair for the show.

As the dance came to an end, the girls formed one line in front of the stage. Myra was so deep in her thoughts that she lost her place. She was facing the left side of the auditorium.

"Myra," Ms. Martínez said gently, "this is a group dance, not a solo performance."

The girls laughed. Myra laughed, too.

Raquel sat in the back of the auditorium and watched them onstage. They looked like they were having so much fun. It brought back memories of the *Dieciséis de septiembre* festivities in Bustamante, Nuevo León. Her teachers had taught her dances like *Jesusita en Chihuahua, Las Zacatecas, La Rueda de San Miguel,* and of course, *El Jarabe Tapatío,* the national dance of Mexico. She almost wished she had accepted Ms. Martínez's invitation to be a dancer.

"All right, let's go over Scene Eleven," Mrs. Frymire called out. "We've made a few changes, so let's see what they sound like." She handed Marco the new script. "You are now El Presidente, Santa Anna."

Marco quickly scanned his lines. Then he read: "*Se ha llegado la hora. Haremos planes para atacar el Alamo por última vez.*"

Arlene Furr turned to Norma Herrera and whispered, "What did he say?"

She whispered back, "He's telling his men that they will make plans to attack the Alamo for the last time."

Arlene nodded.

Izzy: "*Perdóneme, Su Excelencia, pero ¿no sería mejor esperar hasta que llegue Gómez con los cañones grandes?*"

Marco: "*¿Esperar? ¿Para qué? Entran y salen mensajeros de allí como moscas.*"

Norma laughed.

"What did he say?" Arlene asked.

"Shh. Listen."

Marco: "*Ayer entraron treinta y dos soldados a la ciudad de González. ¿Esperaremos a que se fortalezcan? ¡No! Ya es hora de terminar con esto. ¡Atacaremos mañana en la madrugada! ¡Vamos!*"

Raquel clapped loudly. "Yay!"

Mrs. Frymire turned to Mrs. Pruitt and asked, "Did you understand any of that?"

Mrs. Pruitt smiled. "No, but I like it."

CHAPTER THIRTY-FIVE

On Saturday morning, Mr. Cansler and Mr. Watts built the Alamo façade on the top of the stage in the auditorium. They constructed the frame using ten-foot 2 x 4s. Steps on each side were added, separated by a catwalk where some of the performers would stand. Sheetrock panels were carefully nailed onto the frame for the walls. Mr. Cansler sawed out a bell tower, which was then attached to the top.

Mr. Watts spray-painted a long, wide, piece of PVC pipe black. The pipe would serve as the Alamo's cannon. It would be fastened to the top once the Alamo was completed.

Ms. Martínez arrived around one o'clock to check on the progress.

"What do you think?" Mr. Watts asked, gazing proudly at their creation.

"It looks fantastic!" she said. "Except . . . "

Mr. Watts's face fell. "What?"

"Nothing. Well, I guess it doesn't matter." She shrugged. "It's just that the original Alamo didn't have a bell tower."

Mr. Cansler wiped the sweat from his forehead with a plaid handkerchief. "Well, ma'am, I ain't no Alamo expert. I just went by the picture in Billy Ray's history book."

"No, no, please, I'm sorry," Ms. Martínez said. "I think it looks great."

"Well, it should," he barked. "After all the work we done."

The following Monday afternoon, Ms. Martínez, with the help of Ms. Posey and some of the art students, painted the Alamo façade.

First she prepared plaster with a cement base in a large tub. Coarse sand was added to the mixture. After it was ready, the kids spread the gooey substance on the walls of the Alamo. Once it dried, the walls had an appearance of stone. Next, they painted it a cream color with dark tints brushed on to give the walls a more realistic appearance. The door, the columns, the windows, and dozens of minute details were then added.

All the boys who were playing fighters at the Alamo, except for Billy Ray and Marco, got to make their own rifles. Billy Ray wouldn't carry a gun in the play because as William B. Travis, he would lead with a sword. Marco wouldn't be using a weapon at all.

"You're El Presidente," Mrs. Frymire explained. "You'll stand at the back and watch your men do all the fighting. You won't be part of the attack."

"I won't? Man, what a rip."

The boys made the barrels of their rifles out of thin PVC pipes. They formed rifle butts out of cardboard and taped them to the ends. The gun barrels were painted black; the rifle butts were painted chocolate brown.

Orlando Chávez pointed up at the large, black, PVC pipe stationed on top of the Alamo and asked, "Will that cannon be used for anything?"

Billy Ray turned to him and, with a smirk on his face, said, "Yeah. We're gonna use it to shoot Mexicans."

"Billy Ray!" Mrs. Frymire cried.

"Well, that's what it's for, isn't it?"

Part of her wanted to tear into him, let him know what she thought of his narrow-mindedness. But after meeting his father, she accepted that Billy Ray didn't develop that attitude on his own.

"The reason I'm asking," Orlando continued, unbothered by Billy Ray's comments, "is that my dad has a fog machine. He uses it every Halloween to make our house look scary. Anyway, I was thinking that maybe we could attach it to the cannon somehow. Then during the battle scenes, we could release puffs of smoke from it. You know, to make it look like it's firing."

"Orlando, that's an excellent idea," Mrs. Frymire said. "Mr. Gewertz lent me a sound effects CD that has some gunfire and cannon shot sound effects. If your dad will let us borrow the fog machine, it'll add so much to our program."

"Don't forget about my bottle of fake blood," Orlando reminded her.

For the next several days, the students continued rehearsing for the play. By late Wednesday afternoon, they were finally ready.

CHAPTER THIRTY-SIX

The Josephine McKeever Memorial Auditorium had begun to fill with anxious, chatty parents, crying babies, and hyperactive toddlers. Video cameras on tripods were strategically placed throughout the room. A variety of Texas songs wafted from the speakers above as people continued to file in.

"Over here! I found two empty chairs," Blanca shouted, pointing to a row near the back of the auditorium. She and her mother took their seats. Across from them sat Mr. Cansler and a woman whom Ms. Peña presumed was Mrs. Cansler. Their eyes met briefly. Ms. Peña glared at them with a stony expression before turning her attention back to the stage.

Mr. Rathburn appeared and welcomed everyone. He promised them an entertaining and exciting show.

The cafeteria served as the holding tank where the performers waited until they were ready to go onstage. Mrs. Pruitt and Mrs. Frymire helped the students with their costumes. Ms. Martínez fixed the girls' hair. Mr. Watts monitored the noise.

Billy Ray Cansler's aunt had cut and hemmed the front of one of his father's black shirts, leaving the back part to serve as coattails. Billy Ray wore white pants, black boots, and a black felt hat. A brown belt with a sheath that held his plastic sword was wrapped around his waist.

171

Moe Craddock wore a tan, fringed, leather jacket his mother found at the Army and Navy store. John Ahne let him borrow his coonskin cap. John had bought it at the real Alamo mission when he and his parents visited San Antonio.

Marco's grandfather sat at one of the cafeteria tables. He pulled a black felt Napoleon hat with red marabou trim from a bag. When Marco told him he didn't have a hat to wear with his costume, the old man rented one from a costume shop.

"Here, put this on."

Marco slipped on the hat and gazed at himself in the mirror.

"Don't he look beautiful, ma'am?" the old man asked Mrs. Pruitt.

"Yes, he does. He's going to make a wonderful Santa Anna."

"You know, ma'am, me and Santa Anna have something in common."

"Oh?"

"Yeah, he had only one leg, like me."

Marco groaned. "Please, Grandpa, don't start with your one-leg jokes." He turned to his teacher. "Mrs. Pruitt, my grandfather's pulling your leg."

"No, I ain't." Then he smiled mischievously. "But you're welcome to pull mine if you want." He held up his artificial leg.

"Grandpa, no!"

Mrs. Pruitt smiled. "Your grandfather's right. Santa Anna *did* lose a leg. Not a lot of people know that."

"What? You're kidding me, aren't you?" Marco said.

"Nah," the old man replied. "He got it blown off in the war."

Marco looked at him with doubt. "But in all the pictures I've seen of him, Santa Anna has two legs. Shouldn't he be wearing a peg leg or something?"

"It didn't happen at the Alamo, boy," the old man said. "It happened a couple of years later. Right, ma'am?"

"The Pastry War of 1838," Mrs. Pruitt answered.

"See, Marco, France declared war on Mexico 'cause some Mexican soldiers stole some bread from a French bakery. *De una panadería.*"

Marco laughed. "Now I know you're making it up."

"No, I ain't. Ask your teacher. She'll tell you."

Mrs. Pruitt nodded. "Your grandfather's correct."

"Anyway, during the war, Santa Anna got shot in the leg, and they had to cut it off."

"That is amazing," Mrs. Pruitt told Marco's grandfather. "Where did you learn that story?"

"Same place you did, ma'am. From good teachers."

At the back of the cafeteria Mrs. Hornbuckle applied Agatha's makeup. Mascara, blush, eyeliner, eye shadow, and tubes of lipstick were strewn on the table.

Agatha wore a flowing brown skirt with a white blouse and a yellow bonnet for her Susanna Dickenson costume.

Myra Coonrod stopped by her table. "You look very pretty, Agatha." She stared at the makeup on the table. "I don't wear makeup."

"Here, try this." Agatha picked up a soft powder brush. "It's Caribbean Flamingo from the Trudy Carlisle Junior Miss Series." She tapped the brush across Myra's face.

Myra giggled. "It tickles."

Agatha swept a tube of lipstick across Myra's lips. "This is Cinnamon Frost. It'll blend well with your skin color."

Myra picked up a hand mirror and gazed at her reflection. She laughed nervously. "I look funny."

"No, you don't," Agatha said. "You look beautiful."

While the curtains were closed, the choir was herded onto the risers on each side of the Alamo.

Out front, Mr. Rathburn acknowledged everyone who helped with the program, including Mr. Cansler and Ms. Peña. Then, with the pomp and hype of a circus ringmaster, he announced grandly, "Ladies and gentlemen, the seventh-grade students at Rosemont School proudly present to you . . . Miss Josephine McKeever's 'The Battle of the Alamo'!"

CHAPTER THIRTY-SEVEN

The house lights dimmed as the curtains opened. Dramatic, rousing music played while the actors took their places.

"Colonel. Colonel Travis. They're coming after us. Hurry!"

"Whoa there, son. Calm down. What's the problem?"

"The Mexican Army's heading toward Texas. I've gotta warn Colonel Travis."

"The Colonel already knows about that. In fact, we just finished a meeting to make plans on how we're gonna fight them."

"We're gonna fight Santa Anna's army?"

"I'm afraid we don't have a choice."

"But where are we gonna fight an army that big?"

"There's only one logical place. The Alamo!"

"The Alamo?"

"That's right. The Alamo!"

A musical interlude followed. Then, Judy Welch and Karen Ingram began their narration. Karen finished with: "And so, on February 23, 1836, in the town of San Antonio de Bexar, about one hundred eighty-eight brave Texans, who included such men as William Barret Travis, Jim Bowie, and Davy Crockett, gathered together in an old church mission called the Alamo. They converted it into a fort and prepared to fight Santa Anna and his armies, almost five thousand Mexican soldiers, for the right to call Texas a republic."

The actors climbed onstage and delivered their lines with strong conviction and emotion. The audience laughed and clapped at Moe Craddock's humorous take on Davy Crockett.

"I'm Jim Bowie, Colonel. We're mighty glad to have you and your Tennessee boys join us in fighting for our cause."

"Thanks, and the name's Davy. I don't much cotton to that Colonel stuff. Say, I've heard a few tales about ya myself and that toothpick ya carry around your waist. I'm lookin' forward to swappin' tall tales with ya."

"I don't think I'll be up to much storytelling, Davy. I've been feeling kinda poor lately."

"Well, no wonder. Look at ya. Ya look about as cheerful as a turkey on Thanksgivin' Day. You gonna let ol' Santy Anny getcha down? C'mon, Jim, let's find us some señoritas and do some dancin'!"

This was the cue for "Cotton-Eyed Joe."

After the dance, dark, ominous music played. It signaled the first appearance of the Mexican Army. Izzy and Orlando approached the Alamo. Orlando was waving a white flag of truce.

Izzy unrolled a scroll and read a declaration from El Presidente: *"Del cuartel del Generalísimo Antonio López de Santa Anna, Presidente de México, al comandante de los rebeldes americanos. El Presidente manda este edicto: todos los ocupantes de la misión partirán inmediatamente, dejando sus armas atrás. Si esta orden no es obedecida, el Generalísimo tendrá que destruir el Álamo, y todos los ocupantes sufrirán la pena de muerte."*

"See, I told you they wouldn't understand what the kids were saying if they spoke in Spanish," Mrs. Frymire whispered to Mrs. Pruitt when she noticed how quiet the audience was.

"I disagree. Izzy's doing a terrific job. And those costumes look wonderful."

Luther: "Williams, you speak Spanish. What did he say?"

Eric: "He says El Presidente is giving us a chance to vacate the Alamo and for us to leave all our weapons behind. Otherwise, he will destroy the fort and all its occupants."

Billy Ray to Izzy: "Well, you can tell Santa Anna what we think of his generous offer, amigo!" He pointed toward the cannon. The script called for Travis to answer with a cannon shot.

Mr. Gewertz punched the play button on the CD player.

Kaboom!

Mr. Watts threw the switch to the fog machine.

The wrong switch!

Instead of flipping the switch for short bursts of smoke, he accidentally flipped the one for a continuous flow. A steady stream of smoke wafted freely from the cannon's mouth, fogging up the whole auditorium.

Mr. Watts panicked. He kept flipping the switch back and forth, but the smoke continued to pour out. Finally, Orlando ran behind the Alamo and corrected the problem. A short burst of smoke puffed out of the cannon. Mr. Gewertz played the cannon shot sound effect again.

Kaboom!

The Texans cheered loudly.

Moe: "Travis, you have such a fine way with words. I reckon El Presidente won't have any trouble understanding your message."

The choir sang a song called "In Search of the Promise Land."

As soon as the song was over, loud explosions resonated throughout the auditorium. The Mexican Army charged and attacked the Alamo. The Texans fired back. More puffs of smoke billowed from the cannon. The audience hurrahed and whistled as the Texans drove back the Mexican Army.

"Cease fire! Cease fire!" Billy Ray shouted. "They're retreating. Looks like they've had enough for one day. Captain, have your men check the casualties. Get Doc Sanders to help you."

"Colonel! Look! Over at that church. They're raising a red flag."

"I see it. The Mexicans are letting us know with that flag that they're not showing us any mercy, any quarter."

"We've gotta get the women and children outta here. Soldier! Gather 'em all and load 'em into wagons. Let's move 'em out as soon as possible."

Agatha Hornbuckle took the stage. She cradled a toy baby in her arms.

Mrs. Hornbuckle stood up and snapped some pictures. Then she waved her arms excitedly and shouted, "Hi, snookie!"

"Oh, Almeron," Agatha said. "I'm not leaving you. I want to stay."

"Susanna, that's crazy. You saw what just happened. And that was nothing. The Mexicans will attack again at any moment, and it'll be much worse next time. I want you and Angelina out of here as quickly as possible."

Agatha gazed down at her baby. "I'm so worried! The Mexicans scare me. That red flag scares me. But I know you're just as frightened as I am. Everyone here is." She stared at Andy. "Yet, you're staying. You're staying . . . " She turned her eyes back to the baby. "You're staying because you believe in fighting for the freedom of Texas. Well, I believe in that freedom, too. I'm staying, Almeron. No matter what you say, I'm staying."

It was Ms. Martínez's idea to have Agatha carry a doll. Agatha's lines were taped to the doll's chest.

"All right, Susanna, then so be it. I should've known better than to try to talk you out of it. You're a brave woman, and I admire your courage. C'mon, let's go help the others."

As they exited the stage, Agatha's mother jumped out of her seat and yelled, "That's my baby!" Some people in the audience cracked up, but a few others shushed her to be quiet.

"The Widows' Dance" came next. The crowd sat quietly while the girls danced to the slow, haunting tune.

When the dance was over, the menacing-sounding music played again. A parade of Mexican soldiers, led by Freddie Benavides and José Montes who carried Mexican flags, marched down the aisles and climbed up on the stage.

Marco Díaz, as Santa Anna, followed. He strutted down the aisle, full of the self-confidence and arrogance he thought the Mexican president might have projected. Marco wore a black taffeta shirt with red trim and gold embroidery. Along with the gold epaulets and the brass buttons, his uniform also sported various medals and ribbons. Izzy's mother had made the special shirt for him when she learned he was going to play Santa Anna. A pair of black pants and the Napoleon hat completed his costume.

Marco stood at center stage, surrounded by his troops. *"Se ha llegado la hora. Haremos planes para atacar el Álamo por última vez."*

Izzy: *"Perdóneme, Su Excelencia, pero ¿no sería mejor esperar hasta que llegue Gómez con los cañones grandes?"*

Marco: *"¿Esperar? ¿Para qué? Entran y salen mensajeros de allí como moscas. Ayer entraron treinta y dos soldados de la ciudad de González. ¿Esperaremos a que se fortalezcan? ¡No! Ya es hora de terminar con esto. ¡Atacaremos mañana en la madrugada! ¡Vamos!"*

Marco and his soldiers marched up the aisle amid a mixed chorus of bravos and playful jeers.

In the next scene, Billy Ray gathered his forces together. While soft, sorrowful music played in the background, he addressed his troops. "Men, I have some distressing news to tell you. I promised you that we would be getting reinforcements soon. Well, I've just received word that no help is coming. Not in the time needed, anyway. We're on our own."

"What are we gonna do, Colonel?" Herb Williams asked.

"There's not much we can do, friend. There's no point in surrendering. Santa Anna will have us killed for sure if we do. If you wanna take a chance, you can try slipping through the Mexican lines. I won't blame you if that's what you decide to do. But as for me, I have only one choice. If I've gotta die, I'd rather die defending this fort." He unsheathed his sword. "And if any of you want to stay here with me and fight, then cross this line and join me." Billy Ray drew an imaginary line on the stage.

When he was done, Herb said, "Well, I don't know about the rest of you, but here's one life for Texas. I'm with ya, Colonel." He crossed over to Billy Ray's side.

"Count me in, too," Allen said.

"Some of you men carry me over." Luther was lying on a cot because as Jim Bowie, he was supposed to be too ill to walk. He pulled out his rubber Bowie knife. "I don't know how much good I'll do ya, but I'm with ya all the way."

One by one, each Texan crossed the line. Finally, as the background music came to an end, Billy Ray thrust his sword high in the air and shouted, "Victory or death!"

"Victory or death!" his men echoed.

It was time for the final battle.

"For twelve days, the defenders of the Alamo had withstood the continual attacks of the Mexican Army," Alma Crowthers recited. "But in the early hours of Sunday, March sixth, Santa Anna's troops stormed the Alamo for the last time."

"The red flag flying over the church not far away, along with the playing of the dreaded *El Degüello*, were reminders to the Texans that no quarter would be given, and Santa Anna had no intention of taking any prisoners," Sylvia Gonzales added.

There was a loud drum cadence followed by a single trumpet solo.

Travis, Crockett, Bowie, Dickenson, and the rest of the Texans rushed out and stood in front of the Alamo.

"What is it? What's going on?"

"They're playing *El Degüello*, the death song. I guess this is it, old buddy. They're coming after us for sure. Well, if we don't make it here, I'll meet ya at the pearly gates."

Billy Ray stood at center stage. He held his sword high in the air. "If this is to be our final battle, let's show 'em what Texans are made of. In the name of liberty . . . attack!"

The CD player sounded a continuous bombardment of gunfire and explosions. The PVC cannon fired off several puffs of smoke. The Mexican Army charged forward. The Texans fought back.

Cameras flashed nonstop. The audience cheered wildly, as if they were at a Super Bowl game and their team was winning.

One by one, soldiers on both sides fell. A final explosion prompted any Texans still standing to drop to the floor.

After all the Texans were "dead," soft music played in the background.

Norma Herrera narrated: "Within forty-five minutes, the battle was over. All one hundred eighty-eight of the Alamo's defenders were killed. A handful of non-fighters survived. These included a number of Mexican women and children, two black slaves, as well as Susanna Dickenson and her daughter Angelina."

Agatha, still cradling her doll, slowly walked across the stage, grief-stricken, stepping over bodies. Finally, she stopped and gazed down at Andy LaFleur. She covered her face and pretended to weep bitterly. Felipe Garza wrapped an arm around her shoulders and escorted her off the stage.

Sniffling and the blowing of noses echoed throughout the auditorium. Even Raquel, who had been sitting in the audience, got choked up.

"Santa Anna, who had witnessed the battle from a distance, now entered the walls of the Alamo to view the destruction up close," Arlene Furr narrated.

Marco arrogantly marched down the aisle, his chin held high. As he climbed onstage, he gazed down and surveyed the carnage. When he saw Billy Ray sprawled on the floor, he couldn't resist. As he passed by him, Marco stepped on his hand.

"Yeow!" Billy Ray, who was supposed to be "dead," screamed. Then he pretended to be dead again.

The audience laughed.

Izzy Peña turned to Orlando: *"Es una gran victoria para México."*

Orlando Chávez faced the audience and said, *"La tristeza es que tantos de nuestros soldados tuvieron que morir por causa de estos rebeldes.* The sad thing is that so many of our soldiers had to die because of these rebels."

"Amen," Raquel said under her breath. Her eyes became watery.

Orlando removed his hat and formed the sign of the cross.

After they exited, all the soldiers, Texan and Mexican, stood. The dancers, the choir members, and the narrators joined them onstage. Together they sang "Texas, Our Texas." While the students sang, the audience rose to its feet, which every proud Texan knows to do whenever the state song is played.

Texas, Our Texas! all hail the mighty State!
Texas, Our Texas! so wonderful so great!
Boldest and grandest, withstanding ev'ry test
O Empire wide and glorious, you stand supremely blest.

As Raquel Flores sang, her heart swelled. A lump grew in her throat. She felt a strong sense of pride.

The pride of a Texan.

The pride of an American.

God bless you Texas!
And keep you brave and strong,
that you may grow in power and worth,
throughout the ages long!

After the audience sat down, Judy Welch recited: "Susanna Dickenson left to tell the others of the tragedy at the Alamo. 'Remember the Alamo' became a battle cry for all Texans as they rallied together to avenge the deaths of the fallen defenders."

"Less than two months later, the Texans, led by General Sam Houston, launched a furious attack on the Mexican Army at San Jacinto," Karen Ingram continued. "Within a few short minutes, the battle was over. Mexico was defeated and Santa Anna was taken prisoner. Texas had won its independence and a new republic was born!"

CHAPTER THIRTY-EIGHT

After the show, the crowds emptied into the hallway as parents tried to meet up with their children.

Rose Adderly, Miss Mac's sister, squeezed her way toward Mrs. Frymire. "That was the most incredible stage production I think I have ever seen, Doris!" she gushed. "The bilingual aspect lent so much authenticity to the show. I don't know what the Mexican soldiers said, but I loved listening to their Spanish. Josie would have been honored to have seen her play presented the way it was."

"Thank you," Mrs. Frymire said. "It thrills me to hear you say that, Rose. I was concerned that you might object to the changes we made in the script."

Rose Adderly smiled. "I'll let you in on a little secret, Doris. Josie presented that play once, years ago. Afterwards, she got a lot of complaints from the parents about the way the Mexicans were portrayed. She had always meant to rewrite it, but she never did."

Out in the lobby, Mrs. Hornbuckle presented Agatha with a big bundle of flowers. "Baby, you were awesome up there. I wonder who'll be the first one to bring home an Oscar, you or Brenda." Then she turned around and started handing out Trudy Carlisle business cards.

Mr. Cansler had to take Billy Ray's sword away from him because Billy Ray was poking kids with it as they passed by.

Marco was looking for Raquel. He had seen her sitting in the audience during the show, and he hoped she hadn't left yet.

Izzy stopped him in the hallway. "My mom's taking us out to eat at La Paloma Blanca. Want to join us?"

"Yeah, maybe. I'll have to check with my grandpa. Have you seen Raquel?"

"Yeah, she was in the auditorium talking to Ms. Martínez a little while ago."

Marco entered the auditorium. He found it empty, except for Raquel. She was standing in front of the stage, gazing up at the Alamo.

"Raquel?"

She jumped, startled. "Hi, Marco. You were fantastic as Santa Anna. I'm so proud of you." She hugged him.

"I wish you had been in it," Marco said.

Raquel bit her lip. "I don't know if you can understand my feelings, Marco. I'm not really sure I do. My dad has accused me of being too bull-headed, *muy cabezuda*. Maybe I am. But I just couldn't do it."

"Hey, don't worry about it." He smiled. "You're not bull-headed. You're brave. You showed that you've got the guts to stand up and fight for what you believe in. My grandpa would call it your badge of courage."

Marco wasn't sure if he would ever return to the boxing ring. But if he did, he hoped he could go into his matches with Raquel's amazing nerve, courage, and determination.

"Funny thing is," Raquel said, "as I watched the play, I felt so . . . so American."

Marco nodded. "Do you think you and your family will ever apply for citizenship? Or do you think you'll move back to Mexico?"

"I don't know. Ever since the immigration rally in Dallas, my dad's been talking about it, but . . . " she shrugged. "We'll see."

"Anyway, thanks for coming to the show."

Raquel grinned impishly. "The only problem is, I left my tomatoes at home."

"Come here." Marco pulled her close and kissed her.

Izzy burst into the auditorium. "Hey, Marco. We're leaving. Are you . . . ? Oh, sorry." He quickly slipped out the door.

They laughed.

Marco looked up at the Alamo façade. His face radiated with pride. "You know what, Raquel? Years from now, when I hear the words, 'Remember the Alamo!' I'll say, 'Remember it? I was in it!'"

Also by Ray Villareal

My Father, The Angel of Death